Goldhearted

Helen Slavin

© Copyright 2023

Other titles from this author

The Extra Large Medium
The Stopping Place
Cross My Heart
Little Lies
After the Andertons
From a Distance
Will You Know Me
To the Lake
Small Miracles

The Witch Ways Series
Crooked Daylight
Slow Poison
Borrowed Moonlight
Crow Heart
Ragged Starlight
Breaking Bones
The Hedgehog Child
The Ice King

1

Bank Holiday Lark I

29th August 1999

Pargeter's had hosted many previous meetings of ruffians, rebels and ne'er do wells. In all its long history it had probably never harboured such a gang of hard hearts as those gentlemen seated around the Lord Lieutenant's high table on this particular August evening.

The club, for such it was, was one of the oldest eating and meeting places in the city. The tottering grandee of a building criss-crossed the centuries. There were four stories at the front, six at the rear. Pegged together with oak, trussed with iron, Pargeter's had weathered the Civil and Second world wars and every skirmish in between. It's dining rooms, not open to the general public, covered three floors and were of every size necessary. A war council in the Proudlove Room; a quiet tete-a-tete with a mistress here in the Garden Room, a book cooking meeting with your accountant in this little parlour off the back stairs.

On this hot August evening the windows were open. White muslin curtains billowed like clouds in the zephyr like breeze. The leaded lights in a pattern of diamonds threw distorted rainbows of light through ancient glass. Downstairs there was a meeting of the City Townswomen's Guild. Upstairs, in the New Room as it was called, dinner was being served.

It was a vast round table, hinting at delusions of Arthurian grandeur. The chairs, high backed, might have doubled as thrones which was in some way appropriate. The chief gentleman among these thieves was one Owen King. Self-made philanthropist and friend to local business and charity. He was a monument to the fact that you could hide in plain sight. Around the table sat his chosen cohort, each with a skill required to pull off the next day's robbery. They had planned. He had strategized. Here, at his side was Ivo Regan. Twenty three. The heir apparent.

They had gathered for a last supper before the job and, in anticipation, the champagne sparkled. If you listened the slight edge of tension might have made the same sound as a knife being sharpened. The men were ready. They were primed.

It had only been whispered about, the Cossack gold. It glinted now in the basement vault of the Cruickshank & Co bank, a venerable merchant establishment on, and here the fates aligned with their geography; King Street. The bank was flanked on one side by the Merchant Adventurers Hall and on the other by the Radcliffe Collection, an art gallery and museum of no particular note.

The dinner had been genteel. Salmon. Steak. There would be Brandy. Cigars. Owen King had looked around the table, at the familiar and trusted faces as he raised his glass in a toast before the sticky toffee pudding.

"This enterprise on which we are embarked." Owen King began. His tenure as Councillor had lent a certain entitled pomposity to his public speaking. "This, gentlemen, will be our Sistine Chapel. Our legacy. Our crowning glory. Our immortality."

It had taken meticulous planning. Some still felt a little doubt, a small voice that warned, it was out of their league.

But, to a man, they were all in.

Tonight, as the dessert china and spoons made a trinkling symphony and there was a low rumble of masculine chat, Ivo Regan thought of all that had come before. There was much to consider.

There were, for instance, those who were absent from this celebration. These were men brought in to fulfil specific mechanical and practical tasks; in this instance it was Cassidy and Trent. They bodged kit and stole cars and, as they might be both blabbermouth or blackmailer they were told nothing of the specifics. They knew nothing of the cossack gold.

A robbery was taking place. That was all they knew. Which did not mean they could not make a criminally educated guess.

Ivo had been assigned watch from the very beginning. He had been taken under Owen King's wing five years ago, choosing an apprenticeship with the businessman over a university place. He was keen. This job offered an opportunity to show his mettle.

"I want you to know their every last quirk and tell." Owen King had instructed him. "Eyes on." Ivo was a young pup, that was how Browne referred to him, but he was trusted.

"You're on the bottom rung of steeple high ladder, kiddo." Kittredge had said at one of the planning meetings when Ivo had spoken a little out of turn. "Don't overstep yourself." And patted him on the back in a patronising if avuncular manner.

As they were leaving, Ivo helped Henry on with his jacket.

"What you have to remember my boy, is that the person on the bottom rung is the one holding the ladder." Henry, gentleman through and through, with his kind smile and his reassurance.

Ivo recalled a morning with Trent in his draughty garage under the railway arches. A scent of oil and heated metal.

"Strengthening the chassis eh? Heavy payload then." Trent had a sly look about him, like, Ivo thought, a fox rifling through a bin. Ivo busied himself assisting with the steels that they had manufactured this morning in Trent's workshop.

"No idea. It's a need to know basis. I don't need to know." He was firm. His eye cast over the work they'd achieved in the last few hours.

"There's a lot of need to know going on for this job." Trent didn't get on with the final bit of welding, he was wiping his hands on his oily rag. "You for instance. I need to know why you're in on it and what the fuck use you are?"

"I'm an apprentice. On the job trainee." Ivo replied, his politeness level just missing the proper mark. Trent sneered.

"Don't get above yourself, lad. You're the errand boy." he said and pulled down his welding mask.

Cassidy and Trent, not previously big pals, were seen several times together in three locations but chiefly the snug at the Talbot Inn on the Whitworth side of the city. They were seen because it was Ivo's job to keep tabs and follow them. The Talbot was off the grid as far as Owen King's usual cronies were concerned, it was too rank and run down and so Ivo's radar for trouble did a double blip. These two were purposely shifting from sight and the day of the job was approaching.

Owen King was impressed with Ivo's vigilance. "You've done well. Keep them in the crosshairs so to speak. Use your judgement. Do what needs to be done."

The frames were strengthened and Trent had fitted them into the bodies of the small fleet of utility vehicles that Cassidy had pulled in. They were kept, three to a lockup in three different locations around the city. Cassidy was completing servicing all the vehicles. Oil drained from sumps, tyres were swapped and aligned.

A week ago they had held the final planning meeting. The core members of the Cruickshank & Co crew were gathered at Owen King's mother's house for her alleged ninetieth birthday barbecue. It had the advantage of being just out of town and surrounded by lawn, mature trees and a six foot high brick wall. The Dower House, as it was called, was one of Owen King's earliest and most profitable property purchases. Ivo thought that when he bought a house he would buy one exactly like the Dower House.

Discussions were discussed. Plans, routes, maps unfolded. A whiteboard was scribbled on and wiped off. The men in the room drank in the information, only Browne making odd little shorthand notes on his hand, nothing that could be translated by an outsider, his own personal markings. Ivo noted them. A curve, a line and a cross in endless repetition making a sort of music score along his forearm. It looked like a tattoo, runic and ancient.

After the meeting there was, indeed, a barbecue and as smoke billowed, Ivo cleared plates and opened beers. He didn't mind. It left him free to thread himself through the gathering, to listen in on conversations. To keep everyone, as Mr King suggested, in the crosshairs.

The champagne was in the fridge and Ivo filled the champagne buckets with ice as Owen crossed the kitchen.

"Can't seem to get hold of Trent." was his boss's opening gambit "You heard from him?"
Ivo shook his head, continued with his champagne prep, the bottles gilded and clouding with condensation as he lifted them out of the high end fridge.

"Where are we up to with his tasks?" Owen asked, taking a sip of his whisky.

"Done." Ivo assured him. He was no longer in the kitchen. His mind had wandered off to the swan shaped pedalo on the boating lake at Openshaw Park and the dank, black water that had claimed the former mechanic. Done.

"Cassidy went radio silent yesterday. Is he up to snuff?" Owen asked "Did he finish the work?"
In Ivo's mind the angle grinder screamed and sparked.
"He finished." Ivo assured him of that. He took the lock up keys from his pocket and handed them over. "All done."
Owen King looked at the keys for a moment. He blew smoke rings that floated up like thought bubbles as he examined Ivo's face. Not a twitch or tremor, no fake smile or false bravado. Direct. Sure. Owen King's heart beat the same rhythm it would beat when he first met his future wife. This young man, was his protégé.
"You, my lad, will go far."

2

Bank Holiday Lark II

30th August 1999

Mick Quinn enjoyed his job as security officer at the Radcliffe Collection. He liked the fact that he got to wander the halls and galleries of the building alone. He could appreciate all the art. That strange picture of the wild eyed horse with some general atop it waving a sword and wearing what looked like a velvet dress had always drawn his eye. There were many naked statues to be appreciated. Mick liked art. The top gallery in particular was his favourite with its seascapes and landscapes, like little time travel windows and handily placed velvet sofas to sit on while you looked. He loved the place dearly. His grandad had brought him here to do sketching. The rattle of pencils in a pencil case always made him think of grandad.

Mick was doing the Bank Holiday shift as a swap with Barbara who was off to see her daughter in Fife. He had no plans, Trish was spending the day with her mother and besides, he'd done a swap earlier in the year for the May Bank Holiday so it was only fair. It was relaxing to wander the building. It was a cool place, windows shaded by blinds to protect the furnishings and art works. He took time to sit in one of his favourite spots so he could look at the General as he called him. It had been his grandfather's favourite painting and he had often told Mick that there was hidden symbolism in such old works.

"That sword is a broadsword." His grandfather had said "Harking back to ancient times and lineage. No one of his time was wielding a broadsword. It's all propaganda." They had spent many an hour looking at The General. Each time Mick saw the painting he saw something new.

For instance, today, he noticed a fox in the edge of the trees in the distant woodland. He got up from his seat to look more closely. The animal was rendered with just a few minor brush strokes and yet, it gave the impression of activity, of watchfulness.

There was a noise. It was not as direct as a bang but it was out of kilter with the day.

"Hello?" he turned. The silence seemed to be holding its breath. He felt his heart pattering.

At the head of the stairs he paused to listen. He could hear nothing but the nothing he could hear felt suspicious. He trotted down the stairs. There was a draught coming from somewhere and a sound of a car passing outside as if a window was open. None were. His preliminary rounds this morning involved checking all doors and windows. He was locked in.

His own keys jankled against his hip as he headed down the next flight of stairs to the basement level. It was store rooms and the old kitchen down here. The draught wafted at him bringing a scent of the cold flags of the kitchen floor and a hot Bank Holiday scent off the street.

The kitchen door was open. It had not been broken, someone had used a key. He hadn't been expecting anyone. He thought about calling out. It could be Lars who ran the cafe but more likely Mrs Marchmont who ran the volunteers. She had a habit of letting herself in, thought she owned the place.

"Mrs Marchmont?" he whispered. The hairs on the back of his neck had begun to prickle painfully.

He turned. A white ghost, that was what he would recall, later, in the hospital, when the police asked him who had hit him.

3

Police Procedure

September 1999

The cctv from the Cruickshank & Co robbery looked like an undersea adventure. This was not on account of the numerous times the tape had been watched and rewound over the course of the last month. The crew had not bothered to take out the cctv because the place was filled with dust from where they had drilled through from the basement of the Radcliffe Collection into the Cruickshank & Co vault. They had taken this factor into account and behaved accordingly. The perpetrators had worn white hazmat suits so that they all looked about the same height in the hazed dust and their faces were obscured, completely and totally, by the boxy visored headgear.

"It looks like the Cybermen." DC Wyngarde joked. "We should call in Dr Who." And laughed. Alone. In the last few days the Chief Superintendent had spent so long smoothing his beard in frustration that he'd worn a bald patch just on the left cheek.

"We've still nothing on the exit strategy?" Detective Chief Inspector Markham quizzed his team. "What about the cctv at the lights at the Cross Street junction? They look back down King Street." They were scrabbling about in the debris of the job and finding nothing but rubble. Detective Sergeant Fox raised his hand.

"They drilled through the basement of the multi storey car park behind which had no cctv and gives onto Deansgate which also has no cctv, and it was a Bank Holiday so there was no one in town to witness it, so their getaway in whatever vehicles was under complete cover."

DCI Markham looked crestfallen.

"You've got to admire the balls of it. The skill set. These bastards have thought of everything." DC Ashford's appreciative grin was frozen by a bank of stern faces. DCI Markham let his glance linger for a second too long in reprimand and then focused once more on Fox.

"Fox. You said you'd grubbed up something. Where'd you get your intel?" he asked with a raised eyebrow, "Is this tattered bit of string worth knotting?"

Fox nodded.

"One of the workmen doing the resurfacing. Noah Nichols. The basement level had been cordoned off all week because of the works being carried out. They got there on this particular morning and all the barriers were put to one side out of the way."

DCI Markham nodded. Fox continued with a slight edge of hope.

"There are tyre prints in the concrete on the exit ramp."

It felt like a gift from the Gods.

4

A Thousand Tyres

September 2000

Fox knocked on the door of the Inspector's office and heard a gruff response. It didn't appear to be words but Fox had been summoned and so he opened the door.

"Fox. What the hell are you playing at?" was the greeting. Fox frowned in thought.

"Diane came down and said you wanted to see me." He had things to do. "If it's about the Zoo burglar I've picked up the trail. Those little toy animals they leave as a calling card are only sold by…"

"Zoo burglar be damned. I want to know what the hell you think you are doing going and harassing that young woman."

Fox was puzzled. Harrassing? Young woman? His contact at the toy shop was Phil, a bearded grandfather.

"I'm sorry I…" his puzzled expression deepened and seemed to infuriate his superior. "Do you know what, you aren't sorry are you? You don't have a clue what I'm talking about do you?"

Fox opened his mouth to respond. He was recalling a young woman he had interviewed yesterday.

"Who gave you the brass balls to intimidate Councillor Jolly's niece? Hm?" It was clear Markham was agitated. "I've had him on the phone half the morning. She was in tears last night and his sister-in-law, her mother, wants your guts for garters."

Fox took in a deep breath.

"She worked in the museum shop at the Radcliffe Collection last summer. For a few months prior to the Cruickshank & Co job." Fox began "I was chasing a possible lead. She was dating Jex Lennox and it seemed possible she could have given him a key to the kitchen door. Unbeknownst or otherwise."

"So, twelve months on are we so desperate to solve this Cruickshank job now that we're accusing young women of being accomplices to it? Is that it? Get a conviction, at any cost? Have you lost your mind? Also…Unbeknownst?"

Fox understood that Markham had had a trying morning. Councillor Jolly was a tough guy. It had also not escaped Fox's notice that both were golf club cronies of local businessman, Owen King.

"I felt it was worth a shot."

"A year on?" Markham made a huffing sound reminiscent of a grumpy badger. Fox was undeterred. He was onto something with Holly Jolly, he felt it.

"She might have recalled something."

"After, I reiterate, a year?" Markham was determined to shut it down.

"It seemed too good a connection. Jex Lennox has history." Fox stated his case. Markham swiped at his beard in his usual gesture of frustration.

"Fox. You're to let this Cruickshank thing go. Move on. Everyone else has. The insurance was paid. No one cares about some lego blocks of Russian gold anymore. Let it go. The trail is dead, it was never alive."

"I pursued the tyres in the concrete. It showed clearly a vehicle heavily loaded…"

Markham swiped at his beard in agitation.

"It went nowhere. A thousand tyres of the same type. No vehicle was ever destroyed or recovered."

"There were three reported stolen in the weeks prior…" Fox had more, he had an incident room in his head just for the Cruickshank crew.

"Fox. Leave it. It's done. Walk away. I said, the insurance paid out. No one cares anymore. They got away with it."

Fox was not happy.

"Mick Quinn lost his eye." Fox stated the stark

fact. Markham could not argue, but he tried.

"And he was compensated."

"He lost his wife too. She left him." Fox stared at him, the two said nothing for a moment. Markham shook his head.

"I know Mick Quinn is your mate, Fox but it is what it is and I'm telling you to leave it alone. Move on. Leave Jolly's niece alone. Jolly wants you suspended. I'm giving you the week off. Got me?"

When Fox returned from a week away he was told he was no longer a detective but would be heading up a new community policing unit.

"Armed with your litter picker eh?" the newly promoted DS Ashford commented one morning as Fox took his high vis vest out of his locker. "Keeping the streets free from grime."

Ashford's laugh echoed down the hallway.

5
Keep Your Enemies Closer

September 2000

The Rides was one of the biggest racing stables in the county. It was also one of the oldest having housed racehorses for the Prince Regent at one point. Or so the local history books would have you believe. The grand estate had had a couple of Derby winners in the inter war years but Owen King had acquired it through a poker debt via his casino in the city. Ivo Regan was one of the first to have a tour of the place.

"The ace of trumps eh? All this on the turn of a card." He gave his triumphal grin, the same one that had graced the local papers when he had broken ground for the new primary school. "I always said that his lordship was not cut out as a high roller. Too sweaty under stress." He had no sympathy for the debtor.

They walked around the buildings, Owen making a list of repairs to guttering and woodwork.

"I need an expert for the horses Ivo. You know anyone?" they were walking out of the last of the stable buildings and crossing under a vast arch and its stopped clock.

"Alexandra Higham." Ivo had already researched and contacted her. "I've spoken to her. She's happy to come along and take a look."
Owen King grinned further.

"You're always a step ahead. You think she'd come and work for me?"
Ivo nodded.

"Be a gentleman." He warned. Owen King's face creased even more, his eyes glittering with amusement.

"When am I not? And the casino job? How do you think that's going?" they were walking, Ivo could see, out towards a paddock. The gallops were in the distance, white fencing chalking a curving line across the green of the landscape. There was one further outbuilding off to the right but they were headed for a small copse of trees.

"I'm enjoying it. It's a good team." He did enjoy the casino job. He was in charge and he liked the night time life of it. It suited him.

"Good. It's a good spot for you. Besides, as you know I like to keep my friends close…and my enemies closer of course." The grin stretched out across Owen's face once again. The shade dappled their path. Ivo felt a little anxiety as they ventured deeper into the trees, hidden from the sight of the nearest stable girl. He was aware how easy it might be to dispose of a body out here. No one would ever find him.

"Anyway enough about that. How's it going? Your other little task?" Owen asked. Ivo was relieved, nothing was amiss after all. He was just required to report back on his Cruickshank crew chores.

"I heard on the grapevine that Hugh Hardacre was looking at yachts down in Southampton. Hope he hasn't been too bloody obvious with the cash." Owen frowned. Ivo smiled.

"He crashed it maiden voyage out to his new place on the Isle of Wight." Ivo said. Owen smiled.

"Nothing gets by you. What else?"
Ivo had all his information in his head, nothing written down ever. He gave Owen the edited highlights.

"Lennox has gone out of county. Shacked up with some New Age woman, reads cards. He's keeping his head down, looking like a waster."
Owen snorted.

"Because he is a waster." He looked to Ivo for agreement. "In his bones, that lad is a waster. He had one purpose in life. Eh?"
Ivo nodded and after a moment silently looking at the

landscape and contemplating how they had got away with the Cruickshank job, he continued.

"Browne's bobbed off the radar but I got a sniff in Glasgow that I'm looking into. Kittredge and Wilding are quiet and far away. Wilding got married. Step daughter."

"Always handy, a stepdaughter and wife."
Ivo nodded.

"Dalton's gone a bit Lord of the Manor lately but nothing too obvious. They've all been careful."
Owen King looked expectant. Ivo held his ground.

"And Henry?"
Ivo gave a sigh.

"I'm on it." He expected disapproval or disappointment. Instead Owen was sanguine. He nodded, slapped Ivo on the back in a paternal fashion.

"I don't doubt you are. Henry is quite the character but I don't reckon he's a match for you." He took a step forward "Right. Enough shop talk. Come with me…want to show you this view."

The trees gathered and then gave out onto the edge of the plain, the land looping downwards, hinting at the ocean it had once been. Beneath them they could see the city and felt smug, masters of all they surveyed.

6

In a Flash

August 2005

Bobbin was not a happy pony. That statement stood for his life in general, not just that particular day in August. He was by far the most cantankerous of the horses offered at Sandra's Stables. He was stocky and stubborn. Until, that is, Daisy Wolfe arrived with her older sister, Bryony. It was an odd quirk of life that Bobbin loved Daisy and Daisy loved Bobbin.

Bryony did not ride. She thought horses were dangerous and her history of escorting Bobbin and her sister around the local lanes and bridleways had not altered that assumption. Bobbin would spook at the sight of a paper bag or sometimes at a flock of goldfinches flitting across the lane. On other days he would not be torn from grazing the brambles in the hedgerows. Daisy would laugh and tug at the reins and say things like;

"BOBbin." Or with more authority still "BobBIN." There was the more amused "Bobbin don't be naughty. Naughty Bobbin." Or, usually with a laugh and a tug of the reins; "Bobbin you're an idiot."

It was left to Bryony, holding the side rein, to make sure he didn't bolt. It had never really been explained to Bryony how she might stop Bobbin if he took off. He was a pony after all. Even Bobbin probably had the top speed of a small van. She'd just have to run very fast. Or find a paper bag.

That day in August it was hot, a heavy oven sort of heat and the lanes winding out from the stables were narrow and partly shady. Even the shade had the warmth of a hair drier. The sky had started out a bright blue, like something from one of those medieval pictures Bryony had seen in one of the galleries at the Radcliffe

Collection. Bees buzzed and bumped in the brambles. They had only meant to spend a couple of hours wandering but Bobbin had been particularly unhelpful today and now Bryony had decided that it might be an idea to walk down to the Weir at Cowslick so that he could have a drink and they could rest from the heat. There was shade there. Sandra was in no hurry to have Bobbin back and Daisy was enjoying the ride because Daisy loved Bobbin. There was nothing else to do today. Bryony was in an odd mood. The summer holidays were drawing to a close and since she had just turned eleven that year, she was about to start her first term at the secondary school. She hadn't much cared for the place on the visit they had made from her primary school. It was big and rowdy and concrete. But, there was no escape. The thoughts buzzed like the bees.

"Are we going home?" Daisy asked, tired and hot. "This doesn't look right. Where are we Bryony?" she was looking out from her mount at the rolling countryside. It was rolling a bit less now. Some hills had started to fold in on them, clustered with trees. "Bryony where are we?" she was agitated, turning this way and that to look in an exaggerated fashion back up the lane. Bobbin was picking up the unease and stepping a little too high. Bryony tugged on the reins.

"Stop it Bobbin." She whispered. Daisy turned on her.

"It's not Bobbin's fault we're lost." She patted her favourite four legged grump. Bryony was struck with a thought that their cat at home, Sardine, was another four legged curmudgeon who fell into purring fits at the sight of Daisy. Sardine sat on Daisy's shoulder as if he was a parrot. With everyone else he was a Morningstar of claws.

Bryony took pity on Bobbin. It wasn't his fault she had to go to secondary school. "No. It's mine. I thought we could take him down to the river. Give him a

drink."
Daisy was delighted.

"Oh yes. He'd love that. He loves the river."
Bryony wasn't sure how Daisy knew this. The last time they had gone round by Riddlestone the pony had freaked out at the thin trickle over the cobblestones at the ford and had to be walked a mile further down to the little stone bridge. Bryony surveyed their surroundings and tried to work out where they were. The hills and the trees were a clue. She just had to think for a minute. The anxiety of school and being lost merged into a soup for a few moments. Bobbin shook his head in disapproval. Wait. What was that? She could just make out the three storey white stucco farmhouse standing sentinel about a mile away.

"This way. We're just at the edge of Newcombe."

It was another half an hour before they were along the bridleway and heading down towards the river. The sound of the water was glassy bright in the still summer air but the sky above them had darkened to a deeper blue, it was, Bryony thought, pushing towards navy and purple and the air was as heavy as a wet blanket. Along the bridleway the hemlock and hogweed seedheads made desiccated fireworks. The air crackled. Bobbin gave a brief whinny and staggered forwards a few steps, agitated. A cold wind rushed over them and the sky darkened further before being scorched by lightning. It was all Bryony could do to hold Bobbin as he whinnied and stamped about.

"You have to get off." Bryony steadied Bobbin and reached a hand to her sister. Daisy, who was 9, did not need to be asked twice. Her small hand gripped Bryony's and she hoiked herself up and over the saddle. There was a brief moment of blind terror when, just as Daisy was trying to get her left foot out of the stirrup, further lightning taunted Bobbin. Daisy's leg twisted and she was falling. Bryony pulled at him with all her body weight, pushed her hip under her sister's tumbling body. Daisy gave a squeal as she freed her foot.

"Ow.Ow.Ow." she was bright faced with pain, her eyes looked up at Bryony and were brave. "It twisted. It'll be ok." She did not let go of Bryony's hand. She reached to pat Bobbin.

"It's alright Bobbin. It's alright. Just lightning." Bobbin seemed to calm under her touch until the sky sheared white hot once more. It took both the girls to stop him running. He was stamping. Daisy soothed him. Her face against his neck.

"Bobbin. Bobbin." Her little sister's words did the trick.

"Let's get in under the trees." Bryony suggested.

"I thought you shouldn't get under trees." Daisy startled as the lightning seared once more.

"That's just one tree. This is loads of trees." And Bryony, taking no messing about from Bobbin, led them further down the bridleway into the cover of the trees. There was a low threatening rumble of thunder. Lightning sliced, the trees pitted with silver light and the thunder now rumbled through their ribcages like a drum. Daisy gave a whimper and she and Bryony held tight to each other, Daisy with one hand soothing Bobbin. His own nickering was a miniature thunder. They walked on. Bryony felt the need to hurry. Bobbin trotted, anxious with Daisy limping a little beside.

"Let's keep going. We can go up past the bridge and over the river and loop back home on Middle Road." She knew where they were. She had walked here many times with their father. The trees would shelter them. The wind rattled the trees.

And then the rain arrived.

It gushed. It lashed. It was like spears and glass. There was water above them and now, in a vast unfurling cloak, on the ground before them. Bobbin reared and stamped at the oncoming wave and Bryony wrestled him round in the narrow confines of the bridleway. They were running to keep ahead of the water but the nettles and brambles were flattened and the water rose out of the ditches to ambush them. It was cold and strong and gathered them up. Bobbin thrashed. Bryony held onto Daisy. Daisy's arms reaching to loop round Bryony's neck because Daisy was not a good swimmer.

"I haven't got my armbands." Daisy shrieked in a practical sounding panic. Tears were welling. Bryony felt like a stone. They were in the water now, her feet not touching. She was still holding Bobbin's reins and he was swimming now or at least afloat, the current with them, carrying them away. There was nothing they could do. Bryony thought her arms would break. What about Bobbin? Get on Bobbin? Leave go of Bobbin? She felt if she let go of the reins they would be done for. She felt Daisy's tears hot on her face. The water cuffed them, pushed them, dragged them on.

Bobbin was struggling. Bryony felt the rein tug at her shoulder, the joint straining. Bobbin yawed in the whirl of the current, a tree limb fallen, its branches scratching at him. In the swirl he gave a frightened whinny. His big bony pony head slammed round to clash with Daisy's head so that Bryony felt it. He was rolling, a hoof lifted. Bryony cried out, she had to let go. As the pony sank she felt how he would drag them under. Her fingers were tangled she wriggled and wriggled them, her other arm locked around Daisy. Daisy was silent, her breath ragged in Bryony's ear. As Bobbin sank the broken tree limb slammed into Bryony and her arm, instinctively, wrapped itself around it. The thoughts pinged unbidden. She could put herself underneath Daisy like a raft. She could hold on here. The tree was helping. The branch here would help to hold Daisy out of the water. Daisy so still and quiet. Bobbin. Bobbin. Bryony kept kicking even though the river could have cared less.

There was the metal bridge ahead. The thin cow

bridge to Hollow Tree farm. It was too high to reach but Bryony could see there was a car. A man. The man on a rope, dangling like a spider. She could hear his voice. A bellow, a rhythmic and methodical sound. What did he say? There was another rope in his hand, swinging round in a lazy circle. She understood. The rope made an arc, the thing at the end, whatever it was, she must catch that. She must catch, she must let go of the tree. She stopped breathing.

Police Sergeant Fox had been on his return journey from a road safety class at the secondary school when the storm hit. The sky had blackened during the cycling proficiency tests and they'd only just made it into the building. As he drove back the rain was a sluice over his windscreen and he was forced to stop in the layby by the Hollow Tree Farm cow bridge.

That was when he had seen the river. The road ahead would be flooded. He needed to get over the cow bridge and now rather than later. With his wipers on full swing he drove, the water in the lane suddenly like the ford at Riddlestone, washing over the tyres. He was aquaplaning as he turned on to the bridge. The ground fell away six or ten feet here to the river valley bed. Already the banks were submerged, a soup of river water rushing. The car rumbled onto the relative safety of the metal bridge. He had the side window open, partly to try and see and partly in case the water surged and he got washed off the bridge.

As he rolled onto the bridge he heard an animal sound, a horse giving out a desperate scream. He turned and through the sheeting rain he saw, in the tide of oncoming water, the grey pony and beside it the two girls, flotsam in the storm surge. He saw where the tree limb churned taking the pony with it. The girls were not making a sound.

Fox was in the back of his car at once. He was already in high vis so the chances were they might see him. He had ropes and kit for his abseiling club night tonight which was probably going to be cancelled. He was quick to harness up, to find the yoga mat from yesterday. Roll. Knot.

The world was water. He could see the girls, marked out by t-shirts of summer orange and bright blue in the wild grey and white maelstrom of the river. Even in the moments it had taken him secure the rope the river had risen perhaps a further foot. It might help them, they would be higher, closer. The one in orange was not conscious, the one in blue had seen him he was certain. He was down now, over the water. Knotted. Roped. Was this even possible? Could they do it. He must believe. His voice boomed out.

"CATCH...HERE. HERE. CATCH." and he lassoed the rope, the mat knotted onto the end of it, letting the girl see the vivid green of the mat "CATCH THE MAT. CATCH THE MAT." He did not consider what he would do if she could not.

|Police Sergeant Fox's bungalow sat on the furthest edge of the village of Little Midham and was surrounded by high hedges. At the front the driveway curved from the gate, the bungalow set back from the road. It was quiet and it was home.

The girls' mother had brought a hamper of food, a homemade fruit cake, a homemade quiche and a welter of specialities from local producers. Honey. Cider. Wine.

"The scotch is from Orkney." She had said and he could see she was struggling with her emotions.

"Thank you. There really was no need...but thank you. Very kind." He found he was moved by the gesture. By the basket and its spotty red teacloth lining.

"I had to thank you properly." Her voice cracked. "If you hadn't." was all she managed to say. Fox shook his head.

"It worked out." He had thought about all the

little things that had to fall into place that day. That he was on his return journey from the Road Safety. That he had chosen that route. That he had been kitted out ready for the abseiling club. That he had the bright green yoga mat. That the little girl, Daisy, had been wearing her riding helmet which had saved her from the killing blow of the horse's storm tossed skull.

"I can never thank you." Mrs Wolfe said, her voice hardly above a whisper. "You saved my girls. There aren't thanks big enough." He thought for a terrifying minute that she was coming in for a hug but she shrugged. "You're our hero. I wanted you to know that." Fox was moved. He understood why she had arrived with the basket of goodies, with the heartfelt thanks and he was eternally grateful.

The papers and the local tv news had covered the story and for 24 hours it had been wall to wall journalists and he was awarded a medal for bravery from the Queen. A few weeks later, when Daisy was discharged from hospital it was all raked over once more as the Lord Lieutenant presented the medal to him in the Grand Hall at the Radcliffe Collection.

Whilst the rescue featured heavily in most local news feeds Fox was not surprised that there was one two page story in The Chronicle which had focused, almost entirely, on his failure to nail the Cruickshank & Co crew. You could not blame the journalist for latching onto the venue for the medal ceremony coinciding with the upcoming anniversary of the crime. It was a big story of how the thieves, unknown to this day, had got away with all that gold. It was syndicated to some of the national tabloids. The journalist was rumoured to be researching a book. Fox did not really care, but today he was thankful for Mrs Wolfe's gratitude and kindness.

The following morning the post brought pizza fliers, a gas bill and a small white envelope. Inside was a plain white card bearing the typed legend;

```
          Happy Anniversary, defective
                  Detective.
                  sCrew you.
                A wellwisher.
```

Fox looked at the card for a long moment. Typed. It was a very basic font, Courier in fact. It might not be printed, it might have been a typewriter. He sniffed the paper. Thought. Sniffed more carefully. There was a distinct trace of something, he could not place it. He took up the envelope and sniffed its interior. It was more distinct inside the envelope.

    At the back of the bungalow was a dining room with French doors giving out onto the secluded garden. Fox entered with the envelope and card and stepped to the sideboard at the far end of the room. He opened the top drawer and took out a box of drawing pins. He moved to the other end of the room and its blank wall. The card he pinned to one side and, with a marker pen, wrote on the wall beside it; *identify scent*. He folded the flap of the envelope and was about to pin it beneath when his eye was drawn to the smudge of a postmark. Another drawer in the sideboard yielded a magnifying glass. Hm. This might take a while. He put the kettle on and cut a slice of Mrs Wolfe's fruitcake.

7

Gambit

2005

The task he had been set was no small one. He understood that. It was easy to suggest you keep your enemies closer but tracking those enemies when they'd scattered to the four winds was a feat.

He felt the responsibility of it very deeply. The bond between the crew was that of mercenaries. Every single person involved had had their role to play and, if push came to shove, loyalty only to themselves. If there were ever days when he baulked at the job in front of him he thought of Cassidy and Trent and their demise. They were pawns.

The thought of a chess game, was prompted, of course by the fact that Owen King already had the piece assigned him. There was a board he used on occasion to try and visualise the movement of the pieces. Ivo himself was the bishop, he thought Hugh Hardacre might be the Rook. Or was Henry the Bishop? Knights? Wade Wilding and Kittredge fitted that bill. No. Dalton. Dalton and Kittredge. It not only amused him to do this, it got his mind ticking.

And then, when a thought came, when he alighted on a quirk or a tell from all his investigations and observations, he would stop the clock and it was time to take action.

Jex Lennox had given him the runaround but he had a bit of leverage with Holly Jolly. He'd got to her, eventually, through her sister, Jilly Jolly who was vengeful about some sibling wrongdoing.

He was careful meeting up, careful how he introduced the subject that she had, in a very small way, been on the Cruickshank & Co crew. The key member in

fact, he told her with a wry smile.
    "That's not fair." Her lip had quivered and it did not move him "You're not being very fair."
Just because now she had a better class of boyfriend. He didn't really push her, it was a gentlemanly exchange. After all he didn't want to draw undue attention or Owen King's ire. She would keep quiet because, he assured her, she was 'an accomplice'.

8

Cruickshank & Co Crew

August 2006

On the Cards

It had not been too long after the Cruickshank job before Jex spotted Ivo Regan had been breathing down his neck and he'd needed to go off grid. He had resisted the urge to splurge any of his Cruickshank loot. Truth be told the gold almost frightened him. He kept the bulk of it in a self-storage unit on the industrial estate and once a week took a look at it. He'd not realised any of its capital, not touched it, it carried not one of his fingerprints. For a while he'd not known what to do with himself. That particular day he was off to see a man he knew at the Broadwater Hall with a view to a new job involving a bonded whisky warehouse.

En route to this meeting he'd seen Regan reflected in a shop window. He turned. Was he there? The street seemed empty of anyone save the little group of Brownies and two mums with pushchairs. But he had seen him. Reflected. Jex looked at the window again. It was Harper's furniture store. Perhaps Ivo was inside the store looking out. Jex felt his heart leap like a salmon as he checked the entrance. No Ivo. He spun round. His mouth was dry. He began to move off.

The only sanctuary was the Civic Centre and its promise of a Psychic Fayre. Jex ditched the idea of the bonded warehouse. Ditched Ivo. Dodged inside.

He'd sat down at the velvet covered table without really thinking. Later, Layla would say that it was Fate that brought him in there. She did a reading for him which snaffled down the last of his current cash. The first card she drew was a cheery little number titled 'The Hanged Man' strung up by his foot. That card still stuck in his head in his darkest moments. Anyway, Layla had a lot of smudgy black eyeliner and wild red hair so she looked a better option than Ivo Regan, prowling the streets.

Jex Lennox hung around until the end of the day and as she'd been closing up he'd helped her take all the stuff out to her car. Oh look, one of the tyres was slashed and some bugger had clipped the wing mirror. Never mind, I can help you out with my van. He had driven her to Wishbury and never left. She was, if she did but know it, his safe house.

It was not his van. He had slashed her tyre. She was not much of a psychic.

Three years on from all that it didn't seem such a safe house. He had a list of chores as long as your arm today. He'd been expected to load and unload the dishwasher and then he'd been called in to assist with the herb rack.

"I think it's jammed." Layla had said. The rack was an old wooden and cast iron airer, original to the cottage, that could be lowered down from the ceiling by an ornate wrought iron pulley. It was supposed to be for airing laundry but Layla loaded it with little bunches of plants from the garden, some of which Jex was convinced were poison. He'd spent half an hour up the ladder with a screwdriver and a hammer fixing the mechanism and changing the rope. As if that wasn't enough he'd been coerced into helping out at the Goblin Fayre out by the Abbey. He'd spent the rest of the morning loading up boxes of faery houses, oracle cards and all the other tat and paraphernalia that she traded in. This was the last round of boxes. In an all out bid to get the tedious job over with he stacked the three remaining ones too high and headed blindly to the door. There was a stony crunch as his foot struck some heavy object and he was flailing forwards. The boxes tumbled and Jex chipped his tooth on the worktop as he toppled. The boxes of faery houses were strewn across the kitchen flagstones, it looked like an earthquake in Pixie land.

"OH MY GOD JEX." He received a shrill and hearty reprimand in lieu of comfort. No one cared that he had chipped his tooth or perhaps broken his toe. He looked around for the heavy object he had fallen over. Ha. There was the culprit.

That effing Foo dog was his nemesis. It seemed to Jex Lennox that every time he turned around Layla's hideous little mutt was looking at him. Layla called him Mr Chi because of the little brass dog tag round his neck which Jex thought was a brand label. The dog sat with a pompous look on his face and had a habit of getting under Jex's feet. It was impossible how he did it. He stood guard, Layla's term for it, by the back door but occasionally Layla would shunt him about, picking him up with a chuck under his china chin and he'd be put in charge of security by the living room door or called on to prop open the French doors in the back sitting room. He was slightly jade green in colour, with bronze markings and made of some sort of stone earthenware that, however hard you tried, wouldn't even chip. He was tempted to lob the stupid ornament through the windows but the thing weighed a ton.

"Go and get that box from…no. Forget it. I can't trust you. Meet me at the van." Layla moaned at him. There was something in her tone of late. She wasn't hinting at marriage anymore and he was beginning to think his time at Thistledown Cottage might be coming to an end. He was thinking that it might come to an end this afternoon. If he boxed clever. He needed some alone time to recover his pocket Cruickshank stash and then he could be off. It wouldn't take much.

The Goblin Fayre was the usual freak show. It seemed to Jex that even if you weren't a warlock or a magister and you didn't believe in all this, it, somehow, believed in you. It seemed as he helped unload and set up that the elf masks at the next stall were all looking at him. The customers too lurched from odd looking thirty year old playgroup pixie women to sinister Goth men with their goddesses in black velvet tow. He was certain. All the signs were there. From the broken faery house to the vengeful Foo dog Mr Chi tripping him up. It was time he left Thistledown Cottage.

"All breakages must be paid for." He growled at a woman in a tie dye ballgown and stripey tights who was manhandling the faery castle. Layla gasped.

"I'm sorry love, he doesn't mean it." But the damage was done as the woman hurried away. Layla put a weary hand to her forehead.

"Jex. She's been here three times this morning."

"Yes. She's fondled the castle every time. She wants it she can buy it. Nearly had the turret off that time."

Layla pinched her lips together. Even Jex, with his limited vocabulary for human behaviour, understood this was a bad sign.

"She always comes around three times and then BUYS something." Layla was despairing. "Oh. Look. Just get lost. Go home Jex. You're a grumpy git and you're frightening everyone."

Jex was torn. This was exactly what he had planned but he did not like her tone.

"He's the original goblin." Said a voice. It was Cara from the Stones and Bones stall next door. She had her little set up of skulls and rocks. He didn't like Cara because she saw straight through him. Great. After this afternoon he'd never have to see her again.

"Make yourself scarce. You can pick me up at five in the van." And Layla dismissed him with a wave.

His pocket gold was hidden in the bottom oven of the disused range in the back sitting room. He was getting sooty and scratched but he didn't care, he could smell freedom. He'd dug out a small suitcase on wheels and was stacking the bars. This was his emergency exit fund. The motherlode was still in the storage unit. He would sort out his next move and then come back to retrieve that. Could he spend a night in the storage unit if he couldn't find a bunk this evening? It was a possibility. He should take his sleeping bag. Ah. Already there were possibilities. He was laughing to himself imagining the look on Layla's face when he didn't turn up at five in the van. He'd like a photo of that. And then there was a hand on his shoulder. Startled, he leapt vertically, high enough he almost reached the herb rack and its deadly dusty cargo. His eyes fell on his assailant and on a reflex, he pulled his knife.

The story about the freak accident in Wishbury made several papers. It appeared, to the coroner, that Jex Lennox had somehow tripped and got tangled into the mechanism of the overhead airer. The victim himself had, only that morning, repaired the mechanism that strangled him. The freshly greased winch and a law or two of physics had led to him being whirled up by his entangled ankle into the ceiling as the rack became dislodged and toppled earthwards. He had been discovered, some hours later, dangling upside down, festooned with dried herbs.
   The Hanged Man tragedy as it became known was notorious for a while and Layla dressed in black lace for mourning. At a time dictated by an osseomancy session with Cara she had a High Priest perform an exorcism in the house. She found that, true to the maxim,

the publicity surrounding Jex Lennox's freak death was very very good for her Tarot business.

9

Prominent Nominals

March 2012

The school, known as Balderstone School when Bryony first started there, had as she moved into Sixth Form, metamorphosed into the Radcliffe Academy. It was a 1950s building and the assembly hall was a grand space with a velvet curtained proscenium stage. There was, at all times, a scent of plimsoll rubber. This morning, rammed with teenagers, it carried an air of the Colosseum about it.

It ought to have been filled with dust and yawns because the assembly today was a careers special. The whole school, eleven to eighteen, was to witness a talk by a local police officer about careers in the force and the pathways available. It had been going according to plan until from the back someone had shouted at Detective Sergeant Fox;

"Show us your medal."
Fox had fobbed the comment off, with an uneasy modesty and continued with the nuances of traffic policing.

"Show us your medal." The voice again, louder and other voices echoing. Bryony Wolfe was in the sixth form and was sitting on a chair to the side of the assembled crowd. Her friend, Shelley leaned in.

"What are they on about? What medal?"
Bryony knew exactly which medal. It had been a number of years since she'd seen DS Fox but this morning she'd glimpsed him, from the sixth form common room, getting out of his car. She had been surprised how affected she was. There had been no reason to keep in touch with the police officer and yet, they were so deeply connected. He had saved her life.

"Show us your medal." Shouted Mr Daniels the games teacher. DS Fox deflected at once.

"Why not show us yours, sir? Commonwealth bronze swimming 400m freestyle no less." And the policeman began a round of applause and gestured to the games teacher to step up to the stage. As the applause roared and the teenagers woofed and whistled there was some exchange of talk between the two men and a nod. The headteacher, Mr Geary, brought the hall to order with his usual growl.

"So. Let's all imagine that Mr Daniels here is what we call a prominent nominal." DS Fox said. Mr Daniels oozed charm.

"It's been said before." As he japed, ignorant of the meaning of the jargon, DS Fox made a movement that was close to sleight of hand. Mr Daniels found himself handcuffed to the leg of the grand piano.

"With my suspect cuffed I now have to read him his rights…" Mr Daniels looked flustered for a minute, gave a suspicious glare to Fox. The crowd of teenagers cheered and barracked as Fox incanted the caution.

"You can't do this." Mr Daniels, deciding it looked better to roll with it, made a mock protest "You can't arrest me officer I've got a Commonwealth bronze."

"Never won gold!" shouted the same wag from the back of the hall. Bryony looked up to see who it was who had spoken. The hall jeered and took up the chant. Never won gold. Mr Daniels looked embarrassed for a beat and then his charming smile spread out across his face and he began to nod.

"I'm not the only one." He winked. His voice didn't seem raised but it was heard everywhere and the crowd quieted a little. What was going on? Even trussed up like a criminal chicken Mr Daniels exuded a predatory confidence and gave a nod and a wink to DS Fox.

"I didn't win gold. Neither did Sergeant Fox here.

Eh? Never did catch the Cruickshank & Co robbers did you? I got away with a bronze medal, mate. They had it away with all the gold."

"That's true. But, in a lawful society, in order to make arrests you have to have reasonable cause and there must be proof. Evidence. The job was carried out with forethought and strategy and left nothing in its wake."

"It left that security bloke with only one eye…Isn't that evidence?"

Mr Daniels had taken on the stance of a tv drama lawyer, leaning against the piano as if it was a court desk and it was no inconvenience to be handcuffed to it. There was a silence. There was some sort of stand-off going on and no one, including it occurred to Bryony, Mr Daniels, knew which way it might go.

"How many millions was it, Sergeant Fox?" Mr Daniels pushed from his slightly hunched over stance. Bryony looked at DS Fox. He looked, not put down, but exhilarated.

"Thirty million pounds." There was a gasp of awe. DS Fox darted suddenly towards the front of the stage. He gestured to a bookcase backed up against the far wall. "If you'd like to pass me the books off that bookcase…" he nodded to the nearest boy "Hand them down the line in a chain. That's it…pass it on…pass it on…Right. Let me show you…" he received the first of the volumes and started to stack them at the front of the stage "If you had gone into the vault at the Cruickshank & Co bank that August Bank Holiday this is what thirty million pounds in gold would have stacked up like." The books piled. Up. And up.

The hall was once again buzzing. Pupils at the back were straining to see what was going on at the front as DS Fox dragged a white board from the side of the stage. He picked a marker pen out of his own kitbag and addressed them all.

"Let's make the case. Right here. Right now. And

I will show you what policing is really about."
He began to draw a tree diagram on the board, the pen squeaking in the expectant silence. He put initials at various branches of the tree starting with OK at the top.

"So. I mentioned the term 'prominent nominals'. I've initialised them for confidentiality but…this…" he initialled in BHH, IR, HH, JK, WW, AD, PB, JL filling the branches of the diagram "This, is the Cruickshank & co family tree. This is the list of the prominent nominals for this investigation…These are the men who did this. And although I know it I could not PROVE it." He wrote proof in capital letters at the side of the diagram. "So. Let me take you through the case."

What followed was Sherlock Holmes in a high vis vest.

By mid afternoon most of the students had forgotten the entertainment. For her part Bryony Wolfe had made a copy of the tree diagram and took notes. It was not just that it was interesting to her, it was that she felt her connection with Fox, that there was something about the day that was meant to be.

DS Fox had saved her life, now he altered her path.

10

On the Beat

2017

It was her first day at City Central and she thought that the fact that DS Fox appeared to be coming down the corridor to greet her was a good omen. He would take her under his wing, teach her all he knew. Just as soon as he'd dropped off that archive box he was carrying.

He walked straight by her. A dark green document wallet slid from the top of his box, the guts of it, an array of punched pockets filled with paperwork, slinked face down onto the floor. He gave an annoyed grunt and halted as Bryony stooped to pick it up.

"Thank you." He said with a harsh smile and not looking at her.

"Back on the top?" she asked, the file was slippery and heavy. Fox opened the lid of the archive box.

"Just pop it in there for me."
Bryony put the file inside. Fox nodded.

"Saved my back. Thank you." The smile was still harsh and he was taking a step forward away from her.

"I'm Bryony Wolfe, sir. Just starting today. You're Sergeant Fox aren't you?"
He halted, his shoulders tensing as if he was waiting for something more, something possibly unpleasant.

"Not after today."

"Not after…? Sorry sir?"

"I'm retiring." He stated the fact.

"Oh, congratulations sir. You…" she began. He held himself up straighter, faced her.

"I'm retiring today." He confessed and looked at the clock on the wall at the end of the corridor behind her

"In…five minutes in fact. So. Anyway. Thank you for your help. Much appreciated." He walked to the stairwell and turned to go down them. As he disappeared out of sight Bryony retraced her own steps. He was at the first turn downwards so that he was facing her as she spoke again.

"I'm Bryony Wolfe, sir." She said again.

"Yes. Report to the duty sergeant. Not the retired one. Ha." He gave a nod and took a step further down.

"You saved my life." Her voice was louder than she intended, the sound echoing off the bare painted walls of the stairwell. He halted, looked up at her. His brow furrowed for a moment.

"Bryony Wolfe?" she could almost see him rifling the files inside his head. He reached the reference at last "Good God, not the river? You and your little sister?" he was pleased but still standoffish. "Not so little now I suppose. When was it? Ten years? No, '05 wasn't it? Twelve years? Is she well?"

"Very. She's a vet, sir. Almost. Studying at Edinburgh."

"A vet and a police officer. You've done well. Well done." And he continued on his way.

Bryony struggled to catch up with him in the car park despite the fact that she had superb fitness.

"Wait…sir…please."

Fox slammed the boot on his car and took a brisk step to the driver's door, his keys at the ready. But he did wait. His eyebrows raised in impatient expectation.

"I just wanted to say thank you." Bryony was not fazed by his manner. She understood the ribbing and ridicule he had faced in his career, despite the courageous river rescue and his uncovering of the notorious Zoo burglar and in the last year, the Hedgerider Horse Killer. Even reports of that story had twisted its angle to his failures on the Cruickshank investigation. He was haunted by that bank holiday deed.

"Ha." He smiled, the smile harsh but edged with what seemed like sorrow "No need. All part of the job. Plus your mother came to see me…brought excellent fruitcake as I recall. She was too kind. Too kind."

"I wanted to thank you. Not just for the rescue but for the school visit you made. When you went through your case for the Cruickshank robbery."

He visibly stiffened, defensive.

"I'm retiring. Today." He was pointed. "Enough is enough." He held up a hand. Bryony was resolute.

"You don't understand. That day. That changed my life. The case you made. Your passion and your thought process. Everything about it, the whole system. Your investigation process. Everything. You inspired me."

He took a step back, his harsh expression fell away and revealed a vulnerable doubt, head shaking.

"No."

"You are why I'm here today, Mr Fox." Bryony said. She held out her hand. "Thank you."

He looked at her outstretched hand. He was still shaking his head. Finally he took her hand, shook it and reached his other hand up to grasp her forearm and reinforce the severity of his greeting.

"I wish I could save you." He squeezed her hand once again, with real feeling and hard enough to crunch the bones a little, his eyes locked on hers. Then he was in the car, the car was sliding by her, driving away. What did he mean? What was that look in his eyes?

About six months later, mired in a job where the system was run by a barrage of idiotic schoolboy bullies, she fully understood retired DS Fox's warning.

11

A Chasing the Deer

2006

Long ago, when his father was still speaking to him, prior to his choice of career over university, he had been to the Highlands. He was almost thankful that the news story about a shooting at Blairlochy had blipped onto his radar. The task he had been set ensured it would of course, but still, it was, he felt, a sign. It had given him an opportunity to mull over some old memories, to consider where life had brought him. After Cruickshank & Co he wondered if his father had been right.

He'd invested in some tweed in Inverness and he'd taken a stroll up to the castle because life shouldn't be all work. He was relaxed, another piece of the chess game moved across his mental board. It was all good.

The credit card in another name and the pre-paid phone had been a good idea. It was useful for these Cruickshank trips. No one could trace him to hotel or B&B and in fact at the moment he was staying in a lodge by the loch, accessible only by a long and winding dirt track. It was private and peaceful and some part of him would be sorry to leave. His official work environment was often busy and cluttered with people and it had been a revelation to come up here and disappear for a week. He had not been too distracted by the scenery however, he had mapped out a possible exit strategy should matters go awry. He'd seen a pine marten.

The wedding was a gift of course. He had not managed to be taken on as an official staff member for the catering at the castle but they were a slap happy lot anyway. It was nothing to put on the regulation black clothing and the black linen pinnies with the Castle logo were hanging up in a utility room with a very poor lock.

They were short staffed as it was and most of the other waiting staff were sub-contracted. A gaggle of busy strangers, so another drew no notice.

The moment he saw the name of the whisky he took it as a sign.

12

Cruickshank & Co Crew

An Eightsome Reel

September 2007

"Well someone's got to talk him off the parapet." The father in law, a stocky balding man in his early fifties was red faced. "You're the best man." And he dumped the job in Ned Browne's kilted lap.

Browne had been off grid for some time. His purpose built low level home in the wilds near Findhorn, would have welcomed a Hobbit but only one with good orienteering skills. The building was invisible from all sides so well did it blend into the landscape with its green roof and larch cladding.

He knew Craig from the gun club. It was a select membership and the club headquarters were part of an estate, Blairlochy Castle. There was a walled garden and a golf range and the main house, which was a turreted castle by the river, was a wedding venue. He had been shocked to be asked to be his best man. It seemed to Browne that Craig got on better with that twat Gideon Breckan.

"No. You don't get it, you are the BEST man." Craig had been rather drunk the evening he'd bestowed the honour. "Gideon…he's a lightweight. A mate. You man…" he patted Browne on the chest "You SAVED me. You saved me." Pat pat pat.

Browne was stone faced, his memory failing to recall any point in history where he'd saved Craig. Bracken rustled in his memory.

They had been on a gun club shoot on another private estate. Gideon twatface had been about to take a shot and as he pulled the trigger Browne had shoved him over. Hard. The gun fell into the bracken, the shot rang out but didn't kill Craig who had been in the line of Gideon's fire.

"You stupid fucker." Browne had growled. He did not help him up, instead reinforcing his scorn of his marksmanship by standing on Gideon's shooting arm until he heard the bone crack. Gideon gave a strangled cry and a crowd gathered in.

"What's going on? Gid, what the fuck is wrong with you?" was as much sympathy as he received from his compatriots.

"He shoved me." Gideon protested, pointing with his unbroken arm to Browne "You broke my arm you bastard." His voice was thin with shock and pain.

"It was the recoil." Browne said and the protesting victim was carted off in a Land Rover. Gideon had avoided Browne as best he could ever since.

"I owe you my life. That makes you a friend. More than a friend…" Craig continued in an awed tone. "A bondsman." He had leaned in close to Browne, his eyes glazed with a cocktail of whisky and the microbrewery ales they had been sampling. Browne could not lie. He was flattered, in fact he was touched by the masculine emotions drooled out over his knitwear. Plus, it was another one in the eye for Gideon fuckingidiottwatface.

His good deed did not go unpunished when, a few months later, he found himself heading to Inverness with the groom and company for the kilt. He was driving in when he thought he saw Ivo Regan on a bench on a banking by the castle. A panicked look in his rear view failed to spot his former colleague but Browne could not shake the fact that it seemed like an omen. He was alert to every passer-by as the wedding group bundled into the kiltmakers. He watched the windows like a hawk, terrified that when he emerged from the dressing room

Ivo might be waiting for him.

Later, when the fathers and brothers and bridegroom had headed off for some bonding lunch nearby, Browne had been enough on edge to linger in town and sweep every street. The figure he had seen had been fleeting, glimpsed through a car window as he drove by. There was no sign of him now. As Browne walked back along the river towards his car he realised he was spooked. It was a reflex from the necessity of having to come into a town. He was on edge. Wary. He had hallucinated Ivo Regan. He needed to get a grip.

His mood had not altered when he arrived home later that afternoon. He felt compelled to take his shotgun and beat his bounds. It was dark by the time he returned to the house, satisfied that no one but grouse knew where he was.

And now, here he was, in said kilt, finding that it was quite draughty up the spiral stairs en route to the parapet. That draught, wherever it was coming from, was bitter. It was clear from the state of this staircase that Blairlochy castle was not in great repair. There was bat guano to dodge and damp mottled all the limewash. As he shoved open the door on to the roof he was caught by the breeze and stumbled. The view from the wall showed where the castle on this side was crumbling into the river.

Craig was sitting on a small rusted cannon, the breeze whiffling up his kilt but he seemed oblivious.

"Nearly time for the ceremony." Browne could not really think of anything more encouraging to say. If truth be told he didn't care much for the bride. She was shrill and brittle and expensive if his radar was anything to go off. Craig had his head in his hands.

"I can't do it. I can't do it." He whined. "I'm lost my friend...I am lost."

Browne was not one for drama. He was half inclined to jump off the castle himself just to get away from all the champagne and tartan. Instead he turned for the creaking door.

"Fair enough." He had to yank the door open, the bottom of it catching on the stone floor of the tower.

"Wait…" Craig had turned to him "Aren't you going to ask me why I'm lost?" he looked bewildered. Panicked possibly. Browne halted by the door.

"You're lost because you've said you'll marry Tasha. You're not sure you're up to the job. She's high maintenance. You're a bit scared of her and marriage might not always be for life these days but lawyers fees for a divorce are. Call it off. Job done." He took a step onto the spiral stairs. He heard Craig behind him.

"Is that it? That's all you have to say about it?" Craig looked flummoxed.
Browne considered for a moment.

"If you don't marry her I'm sure that Gideon has her card marked. He'll pick her up on the rebound with his Aston Martin." He took another step to the stairs. Craig grabbed his epaulette.

"Wait…what?...What about love?" he pleaded, "What about soulmates?"

"What about them? Does she qualify?"

It was late in the evening and the wedding party had moved into the High Hall for the ceilidh. Craig's new father-in-law Grumpy McKee as Browne had christened him, had taken Browne aside for a moment.

"Just thought I'd take a moment to reward you for fulfilling your best man's duties…and I don't mean dropping the ring on the floor my lad…" he had given a particularly hooting laugh. Browne did not like to be reminded of the ring incident. There was something in the glint of the gold band that had unnerved him, brought a flashback of his fear of Ivo in Inverness. The ring rolling on the floor had seemed, once again, ominous. However, he was distracted as Grumpy McKee brought out a particularly ancient looking bottle of whisky.

"This…" he let the light catch the liquid in the bottle. "This is 'Skene Ór. Only five bottles were ever distilled. It was said to be made by the devil himself at the behest of Seaton of Skene. The infamous wizard." Grumpy opened the bottle and grinned "If you believe in such stuff of course."

Browne felt the dinner of poached Hollandaise salmon and asparagus repeat on him. The dessert of tiramisu was lying heavy in his twitching stomach. He needed a drink. The liquor was poured into a tumbler etched with Celtic beasts. Browne raised a toast to, well, at this point in this odd evening, anyone who might be listening.

The glasses were gifts for the ushers and groomsmen. The tables in the High Hall, set about for resting between Stripping the Willow and an Eightsome Reel, glittered with the crystal glassware. The beasts, the more Browne drank, seemed to keep watch, as if the hall was the lodge of some ancient tribe of warriors. He felt like a warrior in this kilt. In fact he might go back to Chisholms next week and order more. Wasn't that the thing about tartan? Wasn't it Scottish camo? Or was that tweed? He would ask. He could go native and no one would ever find him. He clutched at the gifted tumbler, as if it was a talisman for his future.

Had he spilled some? That waiter had been very diligent and filled and refilled his glass and he might recall spilling some. Or had he sat, at some point, in a wet patch? He hoped it was whisky. It smelled like whisky. Not piss at any rate. He was whirling round the dancefloor. He must go to a ceilidh more often. How old was that bridesmaid? Was she Tasha's sister? Was she high maintenance? Or was she the very princess of his heart?

He'd not had much truck with women. He'd had his heart broken into thin shards by Erin when he was twenty and that had been that. Perhaps there was a reason he was at this wedding. Perhaps it was Fate. Perhaps he had drunk too much of that powerful Skene Ór. He was sweating as he leaned in to Craig's father in law and chinked his glass. Grumpy did not look best pleased, looked in fact as if he could not recall who Browne was.

"Skene Ór." Browne shouted like an incantation and drank the rest of the whisky. "What does it mean? What does any of it mean?" he was skirling with the band, his head a reel, his heart a jig. He was talking, about life. Grumpy looked at him.

"It means Gold." He said, clearly taking Browne literally. Browne thought he might be sick.

In the bathroom he saw what a state he was in. He did not drink often, he didn't like to be out of control and now it was too late. He could smell himself, the sweat plastering his head and rolling down his legs. The kilt was heavy. There were, he had been told, eight yards of fabric in a kilt. It reeked and was damp in parts. He must have sat in some whisky. Or some been spilled on him? He'd been dancing so much he hadn't paid attention. Ór. It meant gold.

He splashed his face with cold water to no real purpose. When he entered the High Hall they were starting up the Pride of Erin and a fateful day felt more fateful.

Later someone commented on the fact that the waiter, 'a waiter' for who knew which waiter as they all looked the same, had spilled quite a bit of Skene Ór heritage whisky on Browne. He had pursued him with a bottle, one stolen, it transpired, from the Blairlochy cellar so that now, allowing for Grumpy opening the other one and the one Bonnie Prince Charlie had quaffed two hundred years ago, there were now only two in existence. He had topped up his glass but also the liquor had been splashed and soaked about.

The candle flame was a tragedy just waiting to happen. Browne, in the midst of the Pride of Erin, had gone up like a wick. The kilt's folds had hidden the flames at first until they had a good hold and as they licked, golden, about his sweating body the panic set into the room. One guest saw the now missing waiter throw what they thought was a carafe of water onto Browne. It had turned out it was more whisky. The waiter followed as Browne began his dash for the window. He had, one guest supposed, been trying to help the flaming guest. It was just a tragedy, that the waiter, clearly trying to help, had fallen out of the window with him and the two had plunged down through the night to the cold arms of the river below.

The news ran a story of course. One of the local rags coined the headline; 'MOLOTOV KILT-TAIL' with pictures of the wedding guests in disarray after the event. Teams of divers had been sent to fish out remains. Browne's body was recovered, smothered in kilt remnants like a burnt offering to the river god. The waiter had vanished. The media lauded the anonymous hero, a gallant young man, tragically keen to help.

"He helped alright." Said Craig's Nana Jean knocking the block off her boiled egg as she read the morning paper.

"He set light to the bastard."

13
Charity Case
2018

"He doesn't fancy you, Brainiac." There was a snorting laugh to accompany this nugget of wisdom "He thinks you're a charity case plus he needs someone to take up his slack." The noisy spooning of instant coffee into a daggy looking mug signalled that PC Holt had finished his morning diatribe.

Brainiac was a nickname that had stuck almost from the first. Once Bryony's policing degree had been brought to light it was inevitable. To any brainless buffoon, Brainiac and Bryony were a match made in heaven. Bryony tried to soothe herself with the knowledge that she was indeed a Brainiac and one of a calibre far outstretching most of her colleagues. She had not been prepared for this. She had thought the collective noun for police was 'force' or 'team'. Six months at City Central had taught her it was 'herd'.

She could have rebutted Holt with the fact that she didn't care very much for Sergeant Crawshaw but it was pointless. She'd tried to state the fact several times and been called, on those occasions 'Wolfe whistle.' At least Brandon Crawshaw had trusted her with the road safety group. She felt there was some sort of fate at work in the fact that Brandon had inherited the road safety gig from Fox. She was happy to participate. He was disgruntled with it. He wanted to be hunting down boy racers on the dual carriageway with his speed gun not teaching kids how to not scoot into the path of an oncoming bus. Crawshaw admitted that he had never read the Highway Code.

"We've got these e-scooters with some grant from the Mayoral fund." Crawshaw informed her "Some charity shit that Fox chased up." They were setting up cones for the first session at, in fact, her old secondary school, the Radcliffe Academy.

"You came here?" Crawshaw asked, his eyes twinkling in an off putting manner. It was off putting because it was glaring how fake he was. He thought he was charming. "Well I never, aren't you are a dark Wolfe." He winked. Once again a huge 'fake' bell clanged in Bryony's head. "I came here too but I was a few years above you." He made a sort of clicking sound with his mouth, the kind she'd heard dog trainers use. "I'd have noticed you Wolfe."
There was that in Crawshaw's favour, he did not call her Brainiac.

She began to enjoy the road safety. She was put in charge of all the school classes and was to report to Crawshaw if she needed help. She found herself trooping round to all the schools with her little mock up zebra crossing made out of slippery plastic and her lollipop and her miniature Belisha beacon. There was even a little pedal car for the primary school groups which was fun and frightening depending on who was pedalling it.

She liked the cycling proficiency and road safety for the slightly older kids. She was keen to hone their road sense and even keener to point out the network of bike paths around the city. The e-scooters were dished out by Crawshaw on a need basis. Some of the kids who attended had difficult backgrounds and Wolfe was affected by the fact that Crawshaw, for all his braggadocio, seemed to take an interest in their welfare and domestic circumstances and to care that the scooters went to the right homes. She was surprised, for her part, that some of the scooters were not stolen or traded away.

The first time she realised what might be going on she was not on duty. She had just come from her mum's house and was on an errand to the big supermarket. A lane behind her mother's house led into a small nature reserve called The Willows even though most of the willows had been shorn down to extend the supermarket car park. The building, a clock towered palace, sat on the opposite side of the small, winding river. She and her mother often walked the dog through the Willows. This afternoon she was crossing the bridge when a young lad on an e-scooter seemed to almost crash into a sixth former on the bridge. Bryony stood back to let him past and the sixth former appeared to not even notice the collision, until, that is, he stepped off the bridge and Bryony passed him. He was putting a little silver foil packet into his pocket.

    The next time was a week or more later. This time she was in the Willows with her mother. They had just approached the Pond, choked as it was with weed and crowded with reeds. On the benches at the far side under the shade of the new willow trees there was another e-scooter and a group of girls. The exchange was quick, e-scooter heading off as Bryony and her mum and Biscuit the border terrier rounded the corner. Bryony thought she was becoming tarnished by police work. She was suspicious of everything. This was just mates meeting. The lad on the e-scooter was just a boyfriend, a friend friend, a gay best friend. All and any of the above. It was none of her business.

    Until she was on duty. She was diligent on her beat, walking around and trying to get to know the community.

    "No one cares Brainiac." Said PC Holt "A little short arse like you isn't saving anyone are they? Can't see you rugby tackling a mugger." He began to laugh, PC Havers sitting nearby looked grim.

    "Actually, take that back," he continued, "I'd pay cash money to see you rugby tackle a perp." He laughed so hard as he sipped his drink that coffee spurtled out of his nose. PC Havers stood up to leave the room.

"You're a prick Holt." Was his parting comment.

In all honesty Bryony Wolfe was more than capable of taking someone down. She had trained at Tae Kwon Do from the age of thirteen and she taught a class at the dojo in the old Grafton Mill complex. She mentally discarded the nonsense and headed out on her patrol.

She liked the walk down by the river, looping as it did around the heart of the city. She would have a conversation each morning with the group of drunks who gathered by the Fisher Bridge. It seemed to her that if she made herself a person instead of a passing figure of authority, the people involved were more likely to approach and trust her. If she was Bryony who shook hands and had a natter it placed her as part of the community. The drunks were a chatty lot and she always listened to their small talk.

This morning she was startled to see that the youngest drunk, who went by the name of D'Artagnan had a wide graze on his face. His eye had swollen up a little under its ferocious scratching.

"You look like you've been in the wars." Bryony offered "I could get you something from first aid for that if you want." It looked fresh and raw and a little oozy. D'Artagnan was not the cleanest of this group. His hair looked as if it had never been washed and had something of the quality of a fleece.

"It was a lion." He was matter of fact "One of them lions the drug barons let loose. You know the malarkey. Cute when it's a kitten…"

"Cub." Interrupted Mischka.

"Yeah. Them like. Then it grows up and its….well it's a fucking lion so it escapes. Or they take it up to the plain and release it there. And then it comes back down to town for snacks. I was a snack." He pointed to the mess.

"It was one of them kids on the flying scooters." It was Ciaran who brought them down to earth.

D'Artagnan groaned.

"Oh. What mate? I had her going then. I had you going didn't I?" he looked desperate for the fun. Bryony nodded.

"I was about to call the wildlife officer." She said. D'Artagnan laughed.

"You're worse'n me." The laugh descended into a hacking cough for which he took a shot of whisky.

"Medicinal purposes." He raised the empty glass in a toast.

"Which kids on which scooters?" Bryony had an uncomfortable prickling feeling on the back of her neck that was not the raw finished edge of her security vest catching on her skin. The drunks looked put out and frustrated.

"Oh. They fly along here. The little fighty one come down the ramp this morning and knocked over D. The other day it was the bigger one with the stupid hair, come zipping along and knocks over Romilly from at the cottage?"

Bryony did indeed know Romilly.

"Knocks her clean into canal." Mischka continued the story. "We had to fish her out with pole from washing line."

About half a mile further along the canal, past the derelict ironworks and the signs for the swanky new development of flats, retail and leisure facilities, there was a small lock keepers cottage. It had narrowly avoided being swept into the new development by dint of the fact that the buildings were all Grade II listed, a nifty move on the part of Romilly when she was quite a bit younger. Romilly owned the half acre of land that the cottage, its old stable and garden stood on. The old stable was her art studio, an enormous rooflight had been put in during the fifties when it was a photographic studio.

She served leaf tea from an ancient and, Bryony thought, Spode teapot. All her china was very beautiful and the mood in the cottage was calming and homely. Romilly was an artist of some reknown locally with an exhibition currently at the Radcliffe Collection.

"Well, at least I got all my innoculations." Romilly said as she offered a packet of HobNobs, her staple diet.

"Innoculations?" Bryony frowned.

"Yes. From all the germs in the water. Never mind. Old joke. Anyway yes. The scooter lads have been a bit of a nuisance of late. A careless disregard for pedestrians on the canal."

"You're alright?"

"Me. Oh, yes. I'm a tough old boot. And I was vigilant for 24 hours, made sure I didn't have any Weil's disease symptoms. Or Lyme. Although I don't think I drank any of the water. I was in there just a few moments and it isn't very deep. Mischka and his pal happened by as I was swimming to the steps at the lock. They thought of the washing pole. It's a bugger to try and pull yourself out."

Bryony felt the prickling prickle more.

"Can you describe the kid?" she asked.

"Why? You aren't going to arrest them surely? Just thoughtless." Romilly offered further HobNobs.

"Can you though?"

Romilly described the older of the two chief miscreants. Mischka had called the hair 'stupid' but Romilly was an artist and drew it. Drew a face too. Bryony was very quiet.

"Can you draw the little one. The fighty one?" Romilly laughed and sketched.

"Yes. He is a bit fighty. A little powerhouse. Wonder if he'd sit for me. If both of them might. Hmmm....I feel an idea burbling." She turned the sketch pad to Bryony. "You know them?"

"They're in my road safety group." Bryony said and after about five minutes Romilly stopped laughing at the irony.

The canal path was a through route for the drug drop offs the kids were making. It was hidden in plain sight. Who really looked at a kid on an e-scooter? Bryony Wolfe did. She watched as they made drops in various points on her beat. It was easy for her to wait in The Willows in the shrubs by the Pond and see the transactions take place.
"Bryony?" a familiar voice cut through the herbage. Bryony had just watched Hal of the stupid hair head off back towards the supermarket bridge. Bryony looked down, Biscuit was sniffing at her ankles. She reached down to ruffle his head, it felt comforting after her morning of crimefighting. Or crime watching at any rate.
"What are you doing?" her mother had the sense to whisper and to join her in the hedge "Are you on a stake out?"
She had missed her chance to follow Hal further. Tomorrow she would get the car and wait at the edge of the supermarket car park and see where he went. There was, she understood all too well, someone else at the heart of this. A Fagin, operating his artful dodgers.

Mark, the fighty one, was flying down the canal. Bryony was on the bridge at the ironworks site and had come armed with binoculars. She could see quite a way from this vantage point. He was clearly in a rush, mowing down a Yorkshire terrier in his flight past the Deansgate steps.
"Aren't you going to do anything? You saw him." The owner was in some distress although the dog was

barking fit to bust and seemed unharmed by the encounter. Bryony assured them she was on it and headed after him towards Prestwich junction. She could see Fighty Mark just whizzing over the bridge and heading in the direction of Brawton.

As she neared the junction she saw Hal Hair squizzing down the steps from the next bridge on Tib Street to scoot along towards Brawton too. The prickling on the back of her neck was not the sweat rolling down from the heat of the morning sun.

The Pumping Station café was housed in the former pumphouse at the edge of Brawton. The building was a pretty neo classical number in stone. The pumping machinery for the canal had long been moved to a more practical shed nearby by the Canal Trust and the café had come into being. Bryony often stopped in with her mother and Biscuit. Here the post-industrial sheds and warehouses, the brick built and abandoned factories now styled as waterside living, gave way to green trees and the glimpse of summerhouses. On the far bank was the boundary of the Botanical Garden.

The two boys were meeting with Sergeant Crawshaw. He was there, in uniform, chatting with them and giving all appearances of a jolly and amenable bobby. He walked them a short way along the canal and in the shelter of the Brompton Tunnel he handed over cash.

Bryony was unpopular at the next meeting of the Road Safety club when she commandeered the e-scooters from Hal and Mark.

"Emergency recall?" Hal frowned "What's that?"

"Something wrong with 'em." Mark nodded
"They did this with my mum's car. There was something dodgy about the brakes."
He was happy to take a bike in exchange.

Crawshaw was not happy.

"What are you doing? What recall?"

Bryony lied. It was a white lie because it was being told for a good reason. She had kept an eye on the drug exchange for a few weeks and, since she had no hard and fast evidence and was not assigned to a case, this was the only way she could think of to put some sort of spanner in Crawshaw's drug dealing works.

"It's a safety issue." She didn't elaborate. The best lies should be kept simple. Her heart was doing a samba. She struggled with her poker face. Crawshaw was watching her very intently. He began nodding slowly, sagely.

"It is a safety issue." He nodded "You're right there." he leaned in a little too close. "And you should remember who is running this little group."

Bryony felt uncomfortable. Was this a direct or an indirect reference to his drug running? Was it a threat?

"You are." She hazarded. He gave a wry smile.

"I supervise. But you, Wolfey, you're the one who runs this group. You know all the kids. You do the sessions. You, are up to your neck in road safety aren't you?"

Bryony stood her ground.

"What do you mean by that?" there was a moment of standoff, his eyes locked hers.

"I mean, read the road, Wolfe, and stay in your lane." he winked and walked away.

The bikes, Bryony discovered, did not hinder the boys errands in any way. If anything they made them less noticeable. Just boys, enjoying a bike ride, here and there, across the city.

14
Secure Measures
2008

It seemed Wade had taken Owen King's modus vivendi of 'hide in plain sight' to a mad degree. The leaflet for 'Locksure Systems' had his arrogant face all over it. 'Locksure' invoked a bout of laughter. Wilding had always seemed like a cocksure idiot but he did know his security systems. He'd been an apprentice in the firm that fitted the system at the Radcliffe Collection. Wade had been invaluable to the crew despite the fact the system they'd had fitted was barely competent to protect a domestic environment, let alone a mid-range civic art collection.

You had to give him credit, he had not gone mad splurging any cash and drawing attention. His current home was a reasonable step up from his previous one. It might be time to adjust his opinion of Wade Wilding. A tweak in perspective. Was this a case of transfer of skills? He felt a smile play upon his lips and was surprised at himself. He ought to be taking the task seriously. Remember, this is a chess game.

Back when they were in school, Wade Wilding had been in trouble for strangling a cat. As observations continued on Wade's home it was clear his animal animosity had not mellowed with the years.

From the way he batted that dead dog across that cottage garden, maybe Wade should have chosen cricket as a career.

15

Cruickshank & Co Crew

An Englishman's Home

2008

Despite his name, Wade Wilding did not care for animals. Cats drew particular ire, gerbils and rodents of other denominations were vermin and therefore virulent. Elephants, lions, giraffes; their exoticism did not save them.

"Evolution mate…get with the programme." he proclaimed. In Wilding's eyes, if you were endangered or on the cusp of extinction it was your own fault. It was an unwise soul who raised the topic of pandas.

Given this information an observer could well imagine the hoopy loopy emotional rollercoaster that Wilding was plunged onto when his neighbour's dogs decided that his gate was the best place to deposit their waste. The gate was wrought iron, a bespoke drawbridge forged by a local artisan blacksmith for an executive castle. The poop was brown and slithery with an aroma, that, should it find its way onto the hall mat, was lingering.

Wilding had bought the house five years ago. He and his wife and his, currently at Cambridge university, teenage stepdaughter had outgrown the last semi despite a two storey extension and a conservatory. They had moved to this modest detached with half an acre of grounds in the next town. Their neighbourhood, due to its distance from the motorway junction and the ugly industrial estate was 'a preferred location'. Wilding preferred it, peopled as it was with men such as himself, self-made businessmen who longed for the law to change to allow them to shoot trespassers.

"That law *has* changed." Devlin was just returning from the bar with the round of drinks; gin and vodka for the ladies and pints of the local micro-brewery's finest for the menfolk. Devlin owned the micro-brewery. It was called the Cat's Pyjamas and the logo was a cat, not surprisingly, sporting pin stripe pyjamas.

"I wanted to call it the Dogz Bollox" Devlin confessed wiping froth from his upper lip "...but she wouldn't have it."

"She? The cat's mother?" his wife, Fleur glared and then grinned and chinked shorts with Wildings wife, Maria.

"Ha! D'you see what she did there? My wife, the wit..." Devlin smoochily kissed his wife. "But yeah mate...that law has changed."

"What law?" Maria was confused by the dogs and cats and pyjamas.

"The one governing trespass. You can shoot an intruder inside your home. Self defence. They've broken and entered so all bets are off."

Wilding considered this. Maria and Fleur shook their heads.

"It's true. It is the law." Devlin was convincing. "Obviously you can't pick them off at the gate or anything drastic but...if they overstep the boundaries...Pop." he made a gun of his hand and shot at Wilding.

The next day Wilding was poised with binoculars in the Through Room as Maria called it. He had an all too close up view of Mrs Morris' pug squeezing out a curly one at his gate. The other dog, a tiny, high strung, hairy thing that looked as if it had just watched a horror film in a wind tunnel, was sluicing down the other gatepost with its piss. Mrs Morris had both animals on reel-em-in leads and was currently trying to reel both of them towards the kerb. Wilding would reel that pug in on fast forward. What was she doing now? Not reaching into a pocket for a hygienic bag? No, no sign of a pooper scooper. No, instead she was yapping into her Nokia.

"Enjoying your walkies Mrs Morris?" Wilding greeted his startled neighbour. She had not seen him approach because rather than come down the drive he had manoeuvred along in the expertly manicured undergrowth by the tall boundary wall, only at this last minute, darting out from behind the gatepost. Mrs Morris glared but did not halt her conversation. Wilding fluttered the crumpled Sainsbury's bag.

"Would you care to make use of this?" flutter, flutter, it was making a satisfyingly crispy sound. Mrs Morris lurched back as if struck and tugged the dogs onwards.

Wilding bagged up the dog poo and watching Mrs Morris disappear along Church Lane he turned towards her house.

Hollyhock Cottage had once been three cottages but now they were knocked into one long thin house. Wilding chose the tree nearest the door and tied the bag of dog poo into a branch.

"You need to be careful..." Devlin advised in the pub that evening.

"Why?"

"There's that law on stalking. She could use that on you, 'specially if she catches you with the binoculars. Plus the whole dog doings in a bag in the tree could constitute criminal damage."

Maria put her glass down.

"He's returning her rightful property." Maria stated. "So there's no case to answer."

For Wilding, every day there was some small miracle from this woman he was honoured to call his wife.

Mrs Morris continued to let her dog defecate. Day after day. After. Day. Plots and schemes blueprinted across Wilding's brain. Poop popped onto her windscreen was amusing but not effective. Poop popped through the letterbox proved a point.

Shortly after the postal poop there was an unmistakeable waft of dog shit as Wilding put the key into the heavy, medieval style lock on his carefully wrought gates. Clearly that bitch, and by bitch he meant Mrs Morris and not the pug or the Hairy Herbert, had used rubber gloves to commit the deed.

"Rubber gloves?" the police officer was very junior it seemed to Wilding. He looked as if he might have to cycle home at any moment to complete a GCSE module.

"I think you are missing a 'sir' off the end of that statement." Wilding gave him the full hard man stare. He paid this upstart's wages after all.

"Rubber gloves, sir?"
Wilding glossed over the slight sarcasm. It might not even be sarcasm, this lad could be entirely innocent of such, it was just that Wilding was wound up and seeing slights in everything.

"Yes. Rubber gloves officer, so that she could push the poop into the keyhole without getting dirty hands…..seems obvious.."
The young officer did not look convinced, although fair play, he did look closely at the mess in the keyhole.

"There is no way Mrs Morris is getting her mani-claws dirty. And no fingerprints either." Wilding was pleased with his latest deduction. "It'll have been those blue latex ones."

Wilding watched later, through the binoculars, as Mrs Morris fobbed off the childish and inexperienced policeboy with tears. Wildings fury reached critical mass.

In the end it came down to killing the dogs. Which one to do first? And how? Oooh, the choices seemed endless.

He was surprised at Mrs Morris' lack of security at Hollyhock Cottage. Not only was there no mortice and tenon on the back door it had been left on the latch. He suspected she would be returning soon from her confab at No 34 The Firs, and made his way quickly into the kitchen.

It was a small matter to punch the pug and break its neck. The high strung hairy one just keeled over with some sort of heart attack before he'd even touched it so he batted it across the lawn with a rolling pin. It was rather disappointing. Wilding felt out of sorts for the rest of the morning.

"You'd have felt better about it if it had been a Great Dane and put up a bit of a fight…or one of those massive things that Alec had…what was that?" Wilding was not paying much attention to the ministrations of Maria. "The huge black one like a bear?" she smoothed her lovely hand across his furrowed brow and kissed his ear, an action which brought him to himself.

"Newfoundland." Wilding remembered. She was right. You'd have to properly wrestle a Newfie.

The scream from No10 was audible as far away as Cedar Avenue, so that perked up Wilding's afternoon.

Maria awoke with a start. A glance at the clock told her it was six thirty and Wilding was not beside her. It must be a golf day, so she dozed for a second or two before realising that it was not a golf day. Perhaps his stomach was upset or he'd got one of his headaches because he was never up this early except for golf.

Maria looked in the bathrooms and checked the games room and the little study. There was no sign of Wilding. Maria stood in the kitchen for some moments. Time was standing still, she could feel it, it was waiting for her to catch up with events.

He was in the garden. She found him at last, run over by the ride-on mower. He was lying, like an oversized oily rag, just by the gazebo.

Triple glazing meant that no one in the neighbourhood had heard a thing.

Mrs Morris preferred to walk her new dogs in the direction of The Pines.

16
Officer Down

2017

Bryony had all her notes and wondered whether it might be wiser to burn them. She'd seen Crawshaw meet up with the kids on two further occasions and was certain he was giving them money. She had, in the end, been out of uniform and on her own bike and followed Fighty Mike. All day. So far she'd not managed to see Crawshaw actually hand over any drugs. You could not be had up for giving money to kids.

"Not the best use of a kid's summer holiday, I grant you." When she shared her theories and investigation her mother had not tried to offer advice, she had been listening.

"Although all the bike riding is improving their fitness." Bryony gave a snorting laugh which sounded painfully cynical. Her mother shook her head.

"We can joke but you need to talk to someone at work. Offer them the observations. Let them take it from there. There must be someone senior. Someone investigating drugs."

PC Havers had recently been accepted on the detective course and Bryony decided to approach him.

He listened. He listened very hard. When he spoke he was straight to the point.

"No one likes you Bryony. You're a woman. You're a brainiac. They don't like your diligence. Everyone likes Crawshaw. This case you think you've got on him will rake over shit. Over you. You will come out of it stinking of shit."
Bryony was silent.

"I'm not being unkind."

"You're being truthful." Bryony nodded. "What do I do?" she wished she'd never spoken out to anyone. She ought to have burned the notes. Looked another way.

"Your job." Havers said "And let Crawshaw do his."

Bryony looked at him.

"It's not his job. It's the antithesis of his job. It's his side hustle. He's not undercover here, he's down at the Pumping Station in his uniform handing out cash to kids who do drug drops for him." She was hissing, she could hear herself. What a disaster this was becoming. Why couldn't she shut up.

"There you go. Right there." Havers pointed at her.

"What? Right where?" she was shaking with rage and impotence. There had to be something she could do.

"Using words like 'antithesis'. That's why no one likes you Bryony."

In the end she took time out at home to write up her notes. Her mind roiled with it all. Would pushing this put the kids in trouble? Wasn't it about stopping Crawshaw using the kids? Would the law see it that way? It was too complex.

She walked the length of the canal the next day and stopped in at The Pumping Station for her lunch. She had a baked potato with coleslaw and discovered that the waitress was going out with Crawshaw. This fact emerged when Crawshaw himself turned up and was greeted with a kiss. He did not look best pleased to see Bryony but he could say nothing as a group of lycra clad cyclists were still finishing their lunch. It was only a little while later when they had gone that he approached her table.

"What you doing here?" he was curt and careless. Bryony noted that Liz the proprietor and the waitress,

Aimee made themselves scarce. Bryony, gathering up her belongings, looked down at the emptied plate.

"Lunch." She could hear the slight tremor in her voice and cursed inwardly.

"You think you're so clever don't you?" his voice was low. Liz and Aimee in the kitchen would not be able to hear. "You are very, very stupid." He sounded pitying. The tremor evident in Bryony's voice had now spread its fear into her hands and she clutched at her hat as she took her farewells.

On her way back to the station for the end of her shift she got a callout about a disturbance under the Fisher Bridge, something to do with the drunks there. Since she was so friendly with them all, she could sort it out.

When she woke up in hospital a week and six hours of surgery had passed.

17

Solid Gold Favour

2019

Mick Quinn was at home with his eyepatch. Even he did not like to look at the puckered place where his left eyeball used to be. He avoided mirrors. Except once he'd put the eyepatch on. It gave him a sort of lopsided, misguided confidence and although it was only a small part exchange for the eye, he was grateful. The one time he liked to catch sight of himself with his salt and pepper hair and the eyepatch was when he headed over to Adam & Eve, the local salon, to have his hair cut by Sheena. He felt transformed. He made an effort. Twenty years on from the Cruickshank robbery he was keeping one step ahead of himself.

This morning had thrown him and he was keen to get down to the golf club and meet up with his oldest mate for some advice.

They were alone in the bar when Mick produced the parcel he had received that morning. Fox, his friend from primary school a hundred years before, looked at it.

"You been on the internet again?" he asked. "What is it this time?" Mick did not have a very successful internet shopping track record. Like the time he bought a rug that turned out to be printed on paper. Or the women's trainers, although truth be told they had been very comfy.

"No. Look at it." Mick glanced around the room, there was no one on their way in. A couple of golf carts were leaving for the first hole. The barman was behind the scenes and there was the sound of a dishwasher being emptied.

Fox leaned forwards. He picked up the oblong parcel.

"Christ it's heavy."
Mick nodded.
"Open it. Open it."
Fox looked at him. Mick nodded urgently at the parcel.
"Just look, where I've ripped it open…look in there."
There was newspaper. Fox unfolded the torn packaging with Mick nodding madly. Fox reached for the newspaper layer.
"What is this? Pass the parcel?" he joked. Mick held up his hand.
"Careful. Don't tear the newspaper. It's important. Trust me."
Fox, carefully, unfolded the newspaper. Inside was a gold bar. The two men were silent for a long time. Time enough for the golf buggy buddies, Ray and Tim, to head off on their way to the second tee.
"You know what this is?" Mick was hushed, church tones.
Fox nodded. He handed Mick the bar, Mick taking charge of it as if it was a hot potato and finally opting to fold it into the ribbed bottom of his golf jumper. Fox looked over the newspaper.
"The Lannerton Echo from…" Fox checked the date "September 2005. That's taking recycling to a new level." He glanced at the newsprint. Mick reached forward and opened out the newspaper. There were three layers. The middle one was a two page spread concerning 'The Wishbury Hanged Man Ritual Killing'.
"Look. Look at this. Read it. Read it." Mick was agitated, shaking. Fox was concerned.
"You alright?"
"Yes. Just. Do me a favour and read it."
Fox read the story of a New Age shop in Wishbury where a local coven were suspected of killing the boyfriend of the owner of said shop in a ritual murder. A photo of the proprietor was foremost, holding up a tarot

card 'The Hanged Man' in one hand and a framed photo of herself and dead boyfriend.

"You know who that is? The boyfriend?" Mick was still whispering, his face pale, giving his salt and pepper hair and his eyepatch even more dramatic contrast. Fox looked at the photo within the photo. It took a minute.

"I think that is Jex Lennox." He said at last. He looked up at Mick. "Can I keep this?" he folded the clipping.

"What do I do?" Mick asked, picking up the remains of the outer wrapping and folding the gold bar back into it. "What do I do? I don't know what to do."

"Think of it as a pension plan." Fox said with a shrug "Someone has done you a, literal, solid gold favour." He reached to finish his coffee. Mick was wired.

"I don't get it. What's it about?"
Fox gave him a direct look.

"Recompense. Maybe." He was throwing out possibilities. Both men were a little uneasy.

"Why now though? I mean, this story…this bloke died fifteen years ago. It's an old story. Why now?" Fox sipped more coffee and shrugged further but said nothing.

"I'm sorry. Cruickshank and all that. This is a touchy subject for you." Mick apologised. Fox reacted at once.

"Touchy for me? Fuck me, Mick. I'm not the one with the eyepatch." Even this exchange was in hushed tones.

"It's the anniversary isn't it?" Mick calmed "I've been thinking about it. Clearly…" he put the gold bar parcel back into his daypack "some other bugger is too." Fox nodded agreement.

"But hey, the other thought I had…"

"Two thoughts in one day Mick, watch yourself…" Fox grinned.

"Seriously. This is a clue isn't it? Remorse or recompense or whatever. If this is from one of the gang it could be a lead." Mick was keen. "Isn't this your chance? You could be like that Scotland Yard bloke, spend your retirement chasing them up at last. Your last hurrah."
Fox shook his head.

"No. Twenty years too late for that."

They finished their coffee and biscotti and headed out to the first tee.

18

Little Midham

2019

    The lane was blocked from the junction at Todger's Cross all the way up to the farm gate at Hollow Farm. It was about half a mile, packed solid, and there were spillages. A random bellowing ruckus drifted across the still Spring air punctuated with pips from an impatient horn.
    "I don't know why you're pipping Dale," PC Bryony Wolfe dodged one of the larger cowpats and leaned in at the car window "You know the cows come up here every day. You could have taken Pippin's Corner and been home by now."
Dale pulled a face.
    "Oh very I told you so." She was miffed with herself "I'd lost track of time. Anyway at least I'm behind them."
It was intimidating to be amongst them. Bryony had been caught out one week and been stuck in the car as the cows milled around her. They were hefty creatures, heavy and languid seeming but sizeable. You wouldn't want to argue with a cow. They might throw their weight around if you did.
    It was only a few more minutes before the cows moved on. Bryony allowed herself the small pun in her head. Dale pipped in a cheery farewell as she went on her way and Bryony retrieved her police vehicle, a chunky tyred e-bike, from the ditch where she had parked it.
    She had been staying, the last six months or so, with her mother in her new abode, an old and rambling cottage in Little Midham. The cottage, labelled Drake Cottage, was a labyrinth of rooms and Biscuit loved it. The garden was vast and her mother was in the process

of untaming it.

"It needs rewilding badly." She said as she peeled the lid off the tub of coleslaw "So I'm the woman for the job."
They were sitting in the kitchen with its copper sink, Verdigris and all. The wooden worktops all had a weathered look as if they'd been salvaged from a ship. There was an ancient Aga in a bright powder blue and Biscuit had already staked his claim by its lowest oven.

"Still haven't quite got the hang of it." Her mother confessed. Bryony looked into the pan and nodded.

"It's been simmering a good half hour." She suggested "They might be done."
 And they feasted on the not quite hard boiled eggs.

"To be fair they are delicious. Back at the old place I used to properly overdo them, like rubber eggs really." The toast too was only slightly singed today "I'm getting the knack of that tennis racket gizmo." Her mother confessed.

"How was your day anyhoo?" she asked with only a slight hint of trepidation. Bryony took in a sharp breath.

"Major traffic jam in The Lane."

"Does it have a name, that lane? I haven't noticed."

"Dead Maids Lane." Bryony said. She had looked it up. Her mother pulled a horrified face.

"Very folk horror."
Bryony smiled.

"Matches up with that pub out at the Greater Midham crossroads."

"Oh yes. The Black Dog. Did you find out who was nicking the horse blankets?" there had been quite a to do about a week ago concerning the theft of three Black Watch tartan horse blankets from the local stable.

"It was an inside job." Bryony looked at her

mother who smacked her hand on the table and looked gleeful.

"I told you. I knew I was right. I said it was that bloody goat. You owe me a tenner." Her mother moved to fill the kettle.

"Not exactly Sherlock Holmes." Bryony sighed. She was crunching up the last of her eggshell. Her mother clicked the kettle on and leaned against the sink.

"So anyway, how are you?"

Bryony shrugged.

"Fine. Very fine to be honest. I like it here a lot." Her mother nodded.

"Me too. But?" Her mother knew her very well.

"But." Bryony felt tears well. Her mind rattled a little. "But I don't know what I'm doing. I mean, is this policing? Is this being a police officer?"

There was a long silence.

"Yes." Her mother nodded. "Yes. I'm going to argue that it is. You are part of the community here. Everyone knows you. You, Bryony, not just some random policeperson strolling by."

"But in my latest case the goat was the culprit."

"What's wrong with that? You got to the root of the matter. You solved it."

Bryony looked at her mum and grimaced.

"Alright. That's a bit much, Mum."

"So was being stabbed."

Her mother's words were not untrue. It was exactly what Bryony thought every day, that she was glad to be here. Glad to be alive.

"You're trying love. You care. People trust you. Forget anything else. Community is key."

"But haven't the bad guys won?" Bryony toyed with the eggshell.

"Oh...Bryony." Her mother looked out of the window for supportive inspiration "I don't know what to say."

They sat in silence for some minutes.

"Just think about Detective Sergeant Fox." Her mother said at last "Think how he was laughed at and ridiculed for that stupid robbery. Did it bother him? No. He just kept doing the job. He found the Zoo burglar and that Hedgerider Horse killer that time and most important of all he saved you and your sister. He was in the right place at the right time that day and... He inspired you. And the bad guys didn't win. They never do. Because they are still bad."

Bryony let all the thoughts mulch together. There was some sense in all this. She was still alive and she was making a small difference here. People did come to her. Perhaps she'd change course a little bit and apply to be the wildlife officer. The right place, at the right time. Who knew where and when that was?

19

Horsey

2009

Horse riding had never been his forte. Scratch that, he'd never really had the time or the funds to make it a strength. There was not that much call for it in the City. Once he had tracked down Dalton however, a plan emerged, once more inspired by the chess board.

He'd known a girl once who called the Knight 'horsey' and it had always stuck with him. She'd had, during their chess games, a real affinity with the Knight and he'd been struck at her strategizing. She made the most of that L shaped move. She was canny, a word his father would have used. That relationship had not gone very far, chess as foreplay and no real chance of becoming his Queen. His father would have liked her. He wasn't sure if these were regrets that were building up.

The VIP ticket was not hard to procure. He had connections after all and besides that it was nothing to mock one up. With extra gold of course. It struck him that Leamingworth Castle could have used Wade Wilding and his Locksure Systems because it was a doddle to get into the venue through the restaurant kitchen.

A doddle. Yes, for someone like him, someone experienced and focused on the task at hand.

20

Cruickshank & Co Crew

The Black Knight
2009

Dalton wanted to impress this young woman and so, when the VIP tickets were sent to him, he thought, why not take her to the joust? They'd arrived from a mysterious benefactor, gilt-edged and anonymous. He suspected that someone at the Chamber of Commerce had facilitated the tickets. He'd been talking with Murphy who was at the top table. Perhaps this was a hint that he was headed there. The Castle was not a genuine old school type castle. It was a Victorian gentleman's residence turned, in recent times, into a bougie event spot but it looked more like a castle than the actual local castle. Tooper's Tower, for any fool unwary enough to trudge over there, looked like a skip load of stones had been tipped on a weedy hillside. Murphy and his cronies were always at The Castle. Like Barons. Whenever he had seen them at the white clothed table in the Cosham Room he had been reminded, haunted even by his past. Once, long ago, he had been at such a table, cigar in hand, brandy wafting under his nose. If they only knew. He could out baron the lot of them. If *only* they knew.

The Castle ran a medieval banquet in the evening where there was a haunch of venison and butts of malmsey but Matty Wisheart the vet had not recommended it.

"Bit of a piss up when we went." he grimaced as his latex gloved hand sutured up the wounded fox on the operating table. Dalton was observing, not assisting, that task was down to Kitty.

"The joust is a good idea." Kitty commented, her face doing that crinkling thing it did when she was thoughtful on a topic. "It's romantic. All historical." Dalton observed the delicate and almost telepathic way that Kitty was handing over the surgical instruments. Fate had been unkind and left her one grade short on her Chemistry 'A' level, snatching her opportunity to pursue veterinary medicine. However, she knew her stuff, that was why Dalton had hired her. On the day of her interview there'd been an oil slick at the fishing lake by the steel works. She'd not thought twice about rolling up her sleeves and sharing her own personal cleaning fluid recipe that left the wildlife hospital scented with vinegar and lemon. She was so unlike the previous incumbent, Jess, who had not liked to get her hands dirty, had only wanted to pet the fluffed and the furry and get her picture in the paper.

Yes. Kitty. How old was Kitty did he think? Dalton felt that the trouble these days was that he was basically old enough to be everyone's dad. He could include Matty in that too.

"You think so?" it mattered to him what Kitty thought "That's your woman's take on it?"
Kitty nodded.

"What's not to like? I mean…horses for a start." she performed her dexterous implement handling, monitored the fox's breathing. "I mean, the last bloke I dated was all for a box of wine and a box set of videos. Never wanted to leave the fucking building." she was laughing, lacking in bitterness. "Big boring bastard."

Dalton was outside the edges of the box set revolution in society. He had only just come around to buying a DVD player. He was old school and still read the local paper. Kitty teased him that he would be featured in it soon as the last man ever to read The Leamingworth Chronicle.

"You could take her to the Witch's Hat afterwards." Kitty suggested, glancing up at him from the fox's paw. Matty winced and made a hissing sound as Kitty cut the finished suture for him.

"You could if you've got a spare kidney." Matt said.

"It's lovely inside. I had to use the toilets in there once doing a beer drop with my dad." Kitty sounded dreamy about the Witch's Hat.

"They don't bring you a bill at the end, they just ask for your car keys in part exchange." Matt quipped.

"The Witch's Hat." Dalton was mentally wandering the main street of Leamingworth trying to place the pub. "Is that the pub opposite the Pump House bridge?" he was struggling, the Witch's Hat? The Witch's Hat?

"No. It's not a pub. It's the turrety house on Mill Road. Big gates and a wall, opposite Newbold Gardens." Dalton knew it at once. He called it the Haunted House in his head and had only ever glimpsed it from the end of the driveway. It glittered at night. Of course. Dalton felt the proposed date with Pernilla was falling into place.

He helped Kitty wheel the fox to its quarters, the quiet block at the back of the building. He had bought the creaking old house and its small hamlet of outbuildings out from under a developer. The neighbours and locals had been glad that such an historic and high end property was going to be saved for the nation. They were less than happy when the planning application showed a future that included a wildlife hospital and nature reserve. He was helped by a close relationship with the councillor heading up the Planning Committee, Heather Pountney. She was keen on wildlife and greening up the town. It was thanks to her that they now had the conservation area in The Smalls, the terraced Victorian houses that ranked behind Newbold Gardens; thanks to her that they had not felled the New Wood and the canal clearance project funding was in place. He might have married Heather Pountney except for the fact that he was an idiot.

He had made anonymous and excessively generous contributions to the Smalls and the Canal projects and volunteered to drive the digger clearing the silt from the basin at Top Mill. She had not forgiven him. He understood. Some nights he lay awake thinking that he'd like a genie and three wishes and that all three of them would be Heather Pountney's forgiveness.

She had kids now, three sons. They could have been his sons if he hadn't been such a twat.

The weather forecasters had prophesied their usual gale force plague of frogs for the weekend but the Saturday of the Joust dawned with delicate bronzed pinkness. Dalton took his early morning mug of tea into his private courtyard and watched the birds on the feeder. He was unsure what the dress code was for the Joust. He'd googled it on the internet and seen that most people showed up in tourist clothing, jeans or hiking pants but he felt he should aim for smart casual. After all, those numpties weren't on a date with Pernilla. He had been to the outfitters on Dean Street. The sign said they catered for the 'Country Gent' and they'd been interested in the idea of a joust. His outfit stopped short of chain mail but involved that modern day Country Gentleman's armour; tweed and corduroy.

The items: trousers, a shirt and waistcoat, were both stylish (according to Damien in the outfitters) and also practical. He could easily wear them to work at the wildlife hospital afterwards. There was a cap in a patchwork of various tweeds and he had been told the story of the vanishing gamekeeper and the role it played in the history of tweed. Harris had been pointed out on a map. It was that sort of shop.

He had not asked the price of anything. Thanks to his criminal past he never had to. He did not even falter at the three digit tag on the boots; handmade. The assistants liked him all the better for it.

" 'Course they liked you while they were emptying your wallet." Kitty was helping him on with his jacket. She was holding the wildlife fort this afternoon.

"Here." he handed her the keys to the van. She looked at them dangling from his hand. "Take them." he insisted.

"You're trusting me with the van keys?" she was disbelieving. He put the keys into her hand, folded her fingers over them. Her funny little stumpy looking fingers that cradled fox cubs and set bones in the wings of birds.

"It smells of dog in here." Pernilla tugged her suede waterfall jacket closer around her silk shirt and with her long, professionally manicured fingers, dusted off the passenger seat. She examined her hand. "Are there hairs?" she looked forensically at the upholstery.

"No. I hoovered." Dalton grinned. He was prepared.

"Is it your dog? Do you have a dog?" Pernilla pulled her seat belt as if it might be a poisonous snake.

Dalton had two dogs, Dastardly and Muttley. They were big hounds of mixed and boisterous parentage and he foresaw them eating Pernilla as a snack. She was quite bony he noticed, as she folded her legs together. Her knees strained against the dark blue denim of her designer jeans. There was a hint of lacy bra beneath the slinky silk of her shirt and he was pleased he was not the only one who had bothered to dress up.

As he put the car into gear his mind reached forwards to the candlelit dinner they would enjoy at the Witch's Hat and later still he would show her the four poster bed in the master suite, the one he'd never slept in.

The Medieval event was busy and scented with doughnuts and burger. Today The Castle restaurant was cordoned off for a wedding. Dalton had thought ahead and brought a picnic basket all loaded up with champagne and smoked salmon.

"I hate smoked salmon." Pernilla did not stand on ceremony, wrinkling her plastic surgery perfected nose.

Were her boobs real? Dalton wondered. They were very pert. Alarmingly perty and severe. Harnessed in the prison of that lacy bra.

"Stop looking at my tits." Pernilla said "There's no glasses for the champagne." she rootled about some more in the boot of the car and came up blank. She shrugged and put the champagne down. Her arms folded as she rested her small bottom on the edge of the car. Was it even a real bottom? Dalton began to be troubled by his doubts. This day was not panning out the way he had wanted. Time was when he could have pulled this off. Time, was a bugger.

She did not care for walking. It was not just a question of distance but the soft ground, the lawns, the general outside nature of the castle.

Their tickets were timed for the late afternoon session and so they took a tour of the castle first.

"Boring as fuck."
And sat through an impressive falconry display.

"He's basically got a handbag full of dead chicks." Pernilla noted in a particularly loud voice. Heads turned. "It's repulsive." she let the falconer continue for a moment or so more before commenting "It looks cruel. Look at him all done up in his BDSM and his little eagle gimp mask."
Bells tinkled.

Dalton was uncomfortable, not just because of what she was saying but because he was thinking of Kitty, her hands around the ribcage of a kestrel as she ringed its foot.

In his mind this day was about jousting and chivalry. This, to Dalton's way of thinking, was a date unlike the run of the mill dinner at a restaurant or the more pointless still cinema/theatre scenario where you were unable to chat and get to know each other. It was all backfiring. What he was learning about Pernilla was that he didn't like her very much.

He considered the dinner reservation. As they wandered through the Crafts and Makers Market, Pernilla disliking that bit of local pottery or taking umbrage against that jar of local honey, Dalton wondered if he could cancel. He was trying to recall if he had put the restaurant number into his contacts. Why couldn't he just ditch her? He could run away down this small alleyway of tents towards the hogroast and lose himself in the crowd. The moment passed.

They were headed to the Tournament Arena. Dalton suggested a toilet break before the festivities commenced.

"Knock yourself out." Pernilla said casting a disapproving eye over the banners cracking overhead.

In the toilets he discovered he had put the Witch's Hat into his contacts. His finger hovered over the green phone call shortcut. Thoughts shuffled and dealt in his head. He swiped quickly across the screen.

"Kitty?" he said when she answered "It's me. Listen, you busy tonight?"

Their seats in the arena were top class with a front row box adorned with a coat of arms. It had cost a pretty penny he imagined, this complimentary VIP champagne package.

"Ugh. Cheap." Pernilla knocked back her goblet of fizz. Dalton knocked his back and considered. Before he had felt flustered and out of sorts. This woman was a mental drain and Dalton was keen to see the joust and lose himself in the ersatz historical nonsense. Ha, already there was swordplay, two knaves in heraldic tabards were clashing and clanging, the sound of steel capturing the restive audience's attention. The bursting blood that fountained from the loser's chest wound drew gasps and cheers. There was a hamming up of a death scene and then the brave squire or whatever he was was carted off. Literally on a cart. More cheering. Except from Pernilla.

The triumphant swordsman rolled out a proclamation, his mike sending his voice booming out, knocking against the castle walls behind them.

"…Let the games begin!…"
Trumpets and drums and a welcome from the commentary box. Local news anchor Alexa White making terrible puns.

It was fun. The best part being that Pernilla's snarky comments were drowned out by the music and the roaring crowd.

"Sir Roger de Coverley and his split second skills there against Sir Isaac Newton. A clash of titans in our wonderful Leamingworth Castle arena today…"
Lances splintered and clashed. More blood spurtled from helmets and through chainmail. The horses were impressive too, big chunky steeds. Dalton had no idea of the breeds and a soft thought struck at him. Kitty would know. He would ask her later.

Sir Galahad and Sir Loin raced about a bit and the hooves thundered. It might be a bit cheesy but the horsemanship and fighting skills were ace. The fizz, however cheap Pernilla found it, hit the spot, Dalton picking up the bottle and swigging a toast to Sir Loin's victory, clunking champagne bottles with the gent in the neighbouring box.

The roaring and cheering rose along with the sounds of confusion from the commentary box as the Black Knight rode into the arena. His horse was black as soot and towering and it seemed a little skittish as wranglers hurried into the arena and attempted to lead it out. The horse and rider dodged and stomped and foam flecks flickered at the bit in its mouth. From the tall wooden gates a supervisor called everyone back and the Black Knight was left to take his entrance cheer. It became, after several moments, a thumping war cry. The black pennant, raised above his armoured head, cracked in the wind. The commentary box was a knock and wheeze of feedback and shuffled papers and half heard voices.

"The Black Knight?" Alexa's commentary partner sounded quizzical and muffled "What?... don't have a black knight?...What are you talking about?...Well why you asking me?...I've no fucking idea who he…" the baffled exchange was quickly shut down for the family audience. The crowd cheered on with bloodlust. It was the most fun Dalton had had in ages.

"Christ." Pernilla sighed and sat back in her seat.

"Who is the Black Knight?" Alexa's too loud commentary burst from the tannoy and took up the slack "From whence did this mysterious warrior ride? Trailing shadows and…erm…darkness on his dark horse of…of…darkness."

The Black Knight's perambulation of the arena and the mess in the commentary box was shifting the mood of the crowd. There was some unseemly dashing about of security guards, harassed looking men were waving their arms about like stressed windmills. They were talking into handsets and headsets in confusion in the backstage area. Dalton watched. Something was up. Sir Gawain was gesturing to the arena gates and the security team were scrambling to let him out. Once in the arena he was off at a brisk canter and for three circuits it appeared that Sir Gawain was trying to chase down the Black Knight. The warrior and his mount were having none of it. The crowd were baying and whooping.

The pace increased, the green knight shouting, trying to cut off the progress of the Black Knight but failing. In a slick move the Black Knight slid his lance into his grip, swinging it wildly so that the black pennant that had fluttered from its tip was whipped into the green knights path, the cloth winding itself around the riders torso and head. His hands left the reins to flail at the cloth and the horse, clearly used to the cue, headed straight for the gates and a swift exit. Already safety teams were swarming out towards the Black Knight as he picked up the pace.

It was wild. It was historic, not to say a bit hysteric. Fuck, Dalton thought, he should have come to this event more often.

Drums beat a tattoo and the safety team swarmed. It was clear now that something was badly awry and the crowd drank in the imminent danger. The Black Knight picked up the pace and re-adjusted his lance. Who was he preparing to fight?

Dalton saw his own face blurred in the polished surface of the breastplate of the suit of armour. Then, hoofbeats, and a thought of Kitty, her hand cradling his own heart as carefully as it might a sparrow, as it pumped out the last of his blood.

21

Stick or Twist

2009

There was a corporate do in the State Room so it was wall to wall black tie. Ivo was not on the casino floor when Henry arrived, he was sorting out a champagne and caviar crisis in the kitchen.

"You need to come Ivo." It was Jono the youngest and frankly the most discreet and clued up of his current shift of security guards. The lad was always impeccably turned out and, if Ivo was being honest, reminded him of himself at that age. Jono was keen, bright and never wasted time so he knew it was a crisis.

By the time Ivo was on the floor of the casino the situation was a small scuffle, a little cloud of tension that lifted and then gave off lightning bolts of hard gestures, an arm raised here, a voice raised there. Already punters were turning from tables and slot machines towards the altercation out of curiosity and irritation and Ivo moved fast to lock it down.

There were three of the security guards circled around the epicentre of trouble. Daniel was taking control, Ivo could see his arms, the biceps stretching the navy wool of his suit sleeves tight as he clamped them around the miscreant.

"No…no please…it isn't what you…This is all wrong." the voice rose above the wall of muscle. Howard in his bespoke Prince of Wales check, Davey in the two piece from Burtons. "Please…" the voice was pleading rather than threatening "If you would just let me…" it was also familiar.

"Henry?" Ivo's voice halted Henry's squirming attempts at escape. Daniel looked to him for instruction and received the nod. Howard and Davey melted into the background as skilfully as their foreman and the gazes from the gaming tables returned to the fortunes of card and wheel.

"Ivo. Thank fuck." Henry looked dishevelled and not simply from his altercation with the security lads. There was a ground in dirt about him, his own suit and shirt looking grubby and lived in. His overcoat, which he now retrieved from the floor, gave off a whiff of damp.

"What are you doing here?" Ivo asked in a cold tone. Henry had come once or twice before on begging missions. The status of his share of the Cruickshank gold, as it was now universally known, was uncertain. He was more than capable of having lost it, and by that, Ivo meant simply misplaced it. Ivo knew that Owen would not tolerate another such visit.

"Dalton." Henry said in a tone that suggested Ivo ought to know what he was talking about.

"What about him?" Ivo spoke quietly, aware of listening ears at the nearest tables, if not the punters then certainly the croupier on 2. Emma? Gemma? Ivo could never recall her name, only that she was a nosey cow.

"What ab...Christ Ivo, don't you know?" Ivo could smell the gin sweating out of Henry's pores, it fuelled his breath, the volume of his voice rising once again. Trust Henry to bring drama.

"Clearly not."
Henry loomed larger than need be, his arms making an expansive and theatrical gesture.

"But Ivo...Dalton? Our compadre. Our crew member...is dead."
The word dropped like a stone and Ivo fought the need to hustle Henry into the nearest small cupboard.

"I'm sorry for your loss." Ivo's tone was sombre. Henry's reaction was incendiary.

"Sorry for my LOSS? WHAT THE FUCK? Did you not hear me?"

Ivo moved forward and with the grace of a ballroom dancer manoeuvred Henry towards a discreet door. One twist of the brass handle and it fell open, Ivo and Henry foxtrotting through it. The door closed behind them. The corridor they had entered was thin and deserted.

"I heard you." Ivo was calm and strong "So did everyone else."

Henry looked panicked, let slip a few unintelligible words that conveyed his inner mental turmoil. Ivo relented half an inch.

"I can see you're upset."

"You can see I'm upset? Upset?" a little floddle of spit flew from Henry's mouth and just missed landing on Ivo's lapel. Henry was lit up again "Ivo, they killed him."

Ivo did not flinch, nor did he breathe for a moment so that he could hear his heart give a brief anxious drum roll.

"They? Who's 'They' Henry?"

Henry was flustered by Ivo's ignorance of the situation.

"I...I don't know."

"Then what are you talking about?"

"I don't know. I heard indirectly. Salter cried off on a visit to the Lodge. Said he'd heard Dalton was gone. I was floored Ivo. Had no clue."

Ivo reached for Henry's arm and began to move him down the corridor to a small office. Henry sagged into the leather chesterfield, the back of which marked the paint on the wall behind it. He wiped his palms across his sweating brow, wiped them on the nearby cushion. Ivo handed him a tissue from a small box he kept on his desk for when grown men cried.

"Ivo, as ever, you are a gentleman." Henry breathed heavily.

"Why are you here Henry?" Ivo's only emotion was suspicion.

"I have nowhere else to go. This is the only connection I still have to the old team, to Owen, to you." Ivo's heart beat a further alarmed tattoo.

Henry was pleading, desperate. "What is happening? First that terrible Jex thing. Then Browne…Wilding…Now Dalton."

"What of it?"

"What of it? What? We need to rally. Someone is mowing us down…Oh God no, how terrible of me, why did I say that, so crass in the light of Wilding. Oh God. What do we do Ivo?"

Ivo took in a deep breath, tried to look unflustered and calm.

"Nothing. It's every man for himself." Ivo shrugged and straightened his cufflinks. Henry was silent, wide eyed.

"I want protection. You need to find out who is doing this before they kill the rest of us."

"What makes you think I can? What makes you think they will?" Ivo had been told he was cold and now he tried to remember it and keep his face a mask. "Lennox has been gone what, four years? You never showed up then with your heart on your sleeve."

Henry gave him a piercing stare.

"That was then. Lennox was a grade A twat. It was no surprise when someone did for Lennox. It was only a matter of time."

"Don't speak ill of the dead." Ivo quipped with another tweak to his cufflinks. Henry suddenly appeared sober.

"Lennox. That seemed like a one off but now Browne and Wilding and Dalton. It's systematic Ivo. This might be Krimchev. Had you thought of that? Krimchev is after us all. He always was a vengeful bastard and King cut him out. Cut. Him. Out." Henry made snipping gestures with his hands. Ivo thought about the last time he'd seen Krimchev and then tried not to think of it.

"You need to keep quiet Henry." Ivo tried. Henry was running off at the mouth now.

"I mean Dalton. The whole Black Knight thing. Leamingworth Castle doesn't have a Black Knight. He just rode off into the distance. Browne liked to ride didn't he? Oh but Browne is already dead. Who rides on the crew? Who is the Black Knight Ivo, who is the Black Knight?"

Ivo wrestled away an urge to slap Henry out of his hysteria.

"Henry." He barked the name. Henry ceased to spiral and looked round, disorientated.

"Mouthing off like this, Henry, just draws attention. Everyone on the crew had an axe to grind that's why when we were done, we were done. Flown on the four winds."

Henry had that sober look once again, despite the fact that his forehead was shiny as plastic with sweat.

"You didn't go far."

"Hide in plain sight." Ivo declared "I've got a good gig here. It would have been stupid to go. It would have drawn attention." He emphasised the last words. Henry licked a bit of spittle from the corner of his mouth and nodded.

"Yes. Very wise. Very sage." He was pensive for a moment and then started "I heard Hugh Hardacre is in Spain. It's every man for himself, I gather that, but someone should get word to Hugh. I might book myself a flight…I should…And Kittredge, is there a way of getting word to Kitt…"

Ivo was quick to move around the desk as Henry stood up, a man of gin and fear-fuelled action. Ivo pushed him back into the seat. Henry was chastened.

"No one is going anywhere near Hugh Hardacre.

Wherever he is. Whatever you heard. If someone is following you Henry they'll follow you to Hugh. Hugh can look out for himself. Same goes for Kittredge. Let it lie Henry."

Henry nodded.

"What you need to do is hide. Whichever bolt hole you've set out from this morning you need to head back there and put the chain on the door. This is what you do when you are being hunted Henry, you don't go around waving a bloody big red flag, you go to earth."

Henry seemed to shrink into the seat.

"You think we're being hunted?" his voice was small. Ivo regretted his scare tactics and in a bid to quiet Henry, reached for the carafe of whisky on his desk and a tumbler. Henry received it gratefully. He rolled the liquid around, staring into it as if scrying.

"Who would do this?" he was calmer now.

"Any one of us, Henry. That's the point." Ivo replied "We're crooks."

22

Fruit Knife

2019

Bryony had organised the self defence class and been pleased at the turn out at the village hall. Several women from the surrounding villages of Piper and Todge's Cross had come along and there was a buzz of chat in the hall afterwards.

"I feel empowered." One middle aged woman had commented after the class. Several others agreed and Bryony was pleased at the age range; some of the women had brought their teenage daughters and even two of the more elderly residents of Little Midham had come along.

Best of all however, was the arrival of Romilly Carew herself, staying behind as the class drizzled out. She was with Drusilla Biggs from Briar House.

"Hello you." She grinned at Bryony and moved in for a hug.

"Hello. What on earth are you doing here?" Bryony felt tears prickle. Romilly winked.

"Oh, I've known Drusilla since the Dark Ages and she dragged me in. Not that I needed much persuasion when I saw who the tutor was. How the devil are you?"

Bryony blinked the tears away and managed a smile.

"I'm great. Loving the country air." She felt an edge of panic, thinking back to the day in Romilly's cottage and the first inkling of trouble. She thought of the hair on the back of her neck. It had not prickled once since she had arrived in Little Midham.

"I'm glad to hear it."

The friend, Drusilla was keen to praise the class.

"We've both enjoyed it. I feel I could kick anyone's arse now." She did a judo chop move. Bryony was uneasy.

"If you remember, Drew, the first rule of self defence is 'run away'." She wanted to make that point.

"Oh I know that but you have to look out for yourself. Why my friend Diana was volunteering in the city last Spring and she was attacked on the canal path and she took a chunk out of the brute's face with a little pearl handled fruit knife she always had in her bag. Stabbed him right in the-" Romilly placed a hand over her friend's mouth.

"Drew. Shut up. I do apologise, Bryony. She has no idea."

"No idea about what?" Drew asked, muffled by paint specked hand.

"I was stabbed." Bryony confessed. Drew looked very upset. Bryony smiled and shook her head.

"Don't worry about it. I'm fine."
Drew was agitated.

"Oh I'm so…Oh…"
Romilly gave a deep theatrical sigh.

"Anyway segueing off into other realms I'm still painting." She smiled at Bryony "I was commissioned to do a portrait of the soon to be Mayor and all round big wig Mr Owen 'I- think- I'm' King." She raised her eyebrows. Bryony laughed.

"Oh yes. I remember him. Very…civic minded. He's the new Mayor is he?" She looked at Romilly who was nodding.

"What a bastard that man is. Christ he couldn't love himself more. I can only think that this is what it must have been like for Holbein painting Henry VIII." She rolled her eyes and grinned. "If that's not giving him too much credit."

"I hope you've put lots of hidden symbolism in."

Bryony said. Romilly shook her head.

"Nope, just painted his pompous face as it truly is. The man's an arse. It's been a real bugger to do and I'm in a bit of a tailspin about whether it's going to be finished in time for the unveiling…" she looked genuinely worried.

"At City Hall?"
Romilly shook her head.

"No. It's going to hang in the Radcliffe Collection. Anyway, they've organised this big red carpet, black tie unveiling, so it has to be ready."

"Perhaps I can pop in on my day off, I can colour in a bit of sky." Bryony offered, only half meaning it. Romilly's face lit from within.

"I would very much like that." She said "How soon can you come?"

23

A Dinner of Herbs

2009

Ivo was on the back foot from the moment Alexandra King, nee Higham, served up the smoked salmon. It had not escaped Owen King's notice that Henry had been in town.

"Did it escape anyone's notice?" Owen looked around the table as if addressing a council cabinet meeting instead of the three of them. Alexandra poured their wine. "The bloke shows up at my casino running off at the mouth about vengeance killings."

"I don't think he said that verbatim." Alexandra dealt with Owen in much the same way she dealt with their horses. "Anyway, I don't know why you're ranting on about it. Ivo dealt with him. With his usual discretion."

Owen looked at his wife.

"Are you in control of this situation?" his voice had risen into a higher register. Alexandra looked at him.

"Someone has to be, you're a bit of a loose cannon." She winked at him. Owen looked mock outraged.

"Anyway, Henry didn't clock on that I'm the Black Knight." Alexandra gave a daring, flirtatious look. Owen's face fell.

"Right. Stop there. Shush. Don't even joke." He was fretful. "A twat like Henry would believe it. Don't even put that nonsense out in the universe." He reached for her hand and kissed it. He turned to Ivo.

"I want him shut up. The man's a grenade."
Ivo nodded.

"I've tried to pick up his trail but Henry is wily. That Cheltenham lead was a busted flush."

"Well be wilier. You know him and his ways. Find him. Shut him up."
Ivo was doing his best. He offered up a different morsel.
"That said. He did give me a tip about Hugh Hardacre. Reckons he's out in Spain." Ivo smoothed a bit of cream cheese over his blini and salmon. "So I'm on the first flight out there tomorrow."
At which news champagne was uncorked.

24

The Patron Saint of Lost Things

2009

The moped delivered an unexpected rush of freedom. He had never cared for Spain, he did not take holidays in general and certainly not anywhere hot. The sun and the coast and the buzzy energy of the vehicle all served to change his mind.

He had gone out to the development at Asta la Vista, ghost town that it was. He could see that the original fishing village had been nothing much and now it was even less. The stark skeletons of the half-finished breeze block built fincas and villas was depressing. A few of the larger properties were rendered and stood eerily white, ready for what he thought was 'first fixing'. On a long stretch of bare scraped dirt advertising hoardings leaned in the wind carrying their faded and tattered sales information about a private golf course.

The breeze was cooling and whistled cheerily through the row of townhouses. He could see what Hugh Hardacre's vision had been. Too late he'd discovered the financial shenanigans that had gone on with Hardacre's business partners. Hugh had been fleeced. Ah, well. No time for a pity party, set a thief to know a thief.

The nun outfit had come to him in a moment of inspiration. He'd been staying at the small, private guesthouse retreat run by the Nuns of the Order of St Anthony. It occurred to him that the area around Hugh's villa was more select, fewer people walking, most people swanning about in air conditioned Beamers and Bentleys. The robe and wimple had been hanging on a washing line in the back garden of the nunnery. When he came into the garden with a cup of herbal tea, not his first choice but the only choice at the retreat, the robe and wimple flapped in the light breeze off the sea.

    Dressed like Mother Theresa and beetling about on the moped he had not felt foolish or conspicuous. He felt refreshed, the robe easily keeping him a degree or three cooler than his twill chinos. He felt free, all Hail Mary, and full of grace.

25

Cruickshank & Co Crew

Hogroast

2010

The day Hugh Hardacre had driven away from the Cruickshank job with the loot in his car, the holdall sat on the backseat where he could view it in the mirror if need be, the car sat so low on its suspension that he had grazed the underside going over a particularly rotund sleeping policeman just outside Preston. That was how he felt these days. Low slung. Ground down.

His dream had been Asta La Vista, a Spanish resort which he had planned to build around a small fishing village further up the coast from where he was now. If he stood on his balcony with a pair of binoculars he could see the remnants of the building works. The little white blocks of the fake fincas and villas, the cranes, abandoned and swinging in the hot Spanish air. He did sometimes look out at this scene, just to bring himself down to earth, to ground his thoughts.

In the midst of the negotiating and investing he had purchased his yacht. It had not proved a good investment from the start. The bloke he had hired as skipper for its maiden voyage crashed into a jetty at the Isle of Wight. It was downhill, or possibly, underwater from there.

He had seen the nun again this morning. He'd been on his way to open for breakfast at the bar and she'd buzzed past on her little moped, wimple in the wind. He'd felt that shiver as if someone had walked over his grave. He'd seen the nun on the moped twice before this week and she seemed to him an ill omen. It was something he carried from his Grandma Edith, who had crossed herself at the sight of any nun whatsoever so that Hugh had always regarded them as malevolent. Certainly this morning she had been a harbinger, his chef had not shown up and so Hugh had had to cover the breakfast shift. He could cook an excellent breakfast, another thing carried over from his grandmother, but the principle of disaster was the same.

The bar was losing money and so here he was, once more, chiselling another bar out of the fireplace at his villa. It was a modest place with a nice garden in an L shape around the house and it had views across the sea. He had a contact in Sitjes that he could use to cash in the gold and as he put it in his pocket and put in another real brick to take its place, he looked out through the windows.

He looked out across the sea and saw a little boat with divers. He was reminded that the Legend of his yacht was that it had been sunk with a cache of gold bars aboard. Divers were always trying to recover this gold. It had been a quarter of his stash, his exit strategy in case of emergency. It had seemed a logical idea to have the bars on board. Ballast and trim were words that swam towards him across the water, in the end weren't gold bars just heavy rocks, shiny rocks, like diamonds if you really thought about it. Rocks and ore. He was not entirely sure that the gold hadn't already been pinched by that graduate student he'd hired as major domo for the summer. A slick and intelligent lad that. Good luck to him, Hugh thought.

What was on his mind now was the time. He was hosting an event at the villa tonight, a gathering of some of his oldest pals. They were other ex-pat businessmen and women, one woman in particular, Lauren Barham, ran a beauty empire and was something of a beauty. The nun's moped buzzed through his head, yes, he understood, he was too old for her. There was quite a crowd, fifty or more, he'd sort of ended up inviting anyone and everyone. It was worth it to network, to let people know he was Hugh Hardacre and he was successful. The main event was a hogroast, another expat business. Laurence reared the pigs at a local farm he'd bought and done up. The animals were treated like royalty and it showed in the meat. Laurence's roaster bloke ought to have been here by now setting up. It was a long, slow and delicious process. As he picked up his mobile to give Laurence a call he heard noise at the gate. There was a sound of gears grinding as Hugh made his way to the front door. Christ what were they doing? The scraping of metal and, as he opened the door, the van wheels whirring. It was trapped between the two stone pillars, one of his gates was hanging off, bent. Jesus, it was a pig in a van, how hard could it be? He'd have words with Laurence about this. Might even get the pig for free off the back of it.

"HOI." He was striding towards the trapped van, the wheels whirring like wasps in jam. Somewhere a gear popped in with a sickening jolt.

The hogroast guests had been told to arrive for eight o'clock and Hugh had been aware when issuing this invite that many of them might not turn up until nine. As the first of the guests arrived, Lauren Barham in fact, she noticed that one of the pillars of the gate had fallen completely over. It was quite the manoeuvre to get around it really even in her Mini Cooper. The gate was sprawled like a drawbridge.

There was music coming from inside the house and a delicious scent of garlic and fennel and roasting pork. Lauren had tried to be veggie but pulled pork was her downfall. It had occurred to her that Hugh, handsome old Hugh, had decided on a hogroast because she had been chatting one day and mentioned her guilty pleasure. What she liked about him was that he hadn't made a crude pork joke. It was one of the things that had made her see him differently. It was easy to see that he was fifty probably, that he was shaven headed and if he was caught off guard he looked a terrifying hard man. It was also comforting to talk to him. He listened. They had conversations. He was handsome and he was Rich with a capital R. Look at that big business venture up the coast. Although Amelie, the colourist at her salon, had told her that he was bankrupt. That that whole project had been flushed right down the toilet and he was only holding onto the bar and villa by the skin of his veneers.

  She knocked on the front door and also tried the bell which she heard ringing out. She waited, stood in the porch and watched as Nick Melville pulled in and tried to manoeuvre his massive red Range Rover around the gate and the broken pillar. No one was answering the door. There was music, perhaps Hugh couldn't hear. He was fifty after all. Probably. Probably deaf. She waved at Nick as he drove his car over the gate, bending it irreparably. As he got out of his vehicle he moved to drag the gate out of the way of the drive, sling it onto the lawn.

  "What are you hanging around here for? Why don't you just go round the back?" he asked in his usual pompous tone. She didn't like Nick so she didn't wait for him to finish locking up the car and straightening up his shirt and his big watch. She headed around the side of the house, through the gate in the hedge beneath the archway of hibiscus.

  That hogroast smelt so good.

As she looked back to see where Nick was, she saw a nun on a moped scoot past the gate and, superstitious, she crossed herself.

26

An Old School Gent

2019

Henry Hallam was out in the garden pruning back the wilder outreaches of the clematis that frothed over his front door. Even to do this task Henry was wearing linen trousers and a cravat with his blue chambray shirt. His clothes, Bryony had noticed, were old but were of good quality. His suits for instance, while often stained with gravy or egg were clearly tailored, possibly handsewn. Judging by the shiny state of his forehead beneath his stylish quiff, he had already had elevenses with tonic and lemon this morning.

"Morning Henry." Bryony was on duty, opting to walk the village streets before heading further afield in the car. Henry turned rather sharply as if startled and his face was a grim mask for a second before he recognised her.

"Ah, my dear. And how are you this slightly overcast morning?" he cast a glance up at the sky. "Think it's likely to pour down later?"
Bryony also looked up at the sky.

"I think the forecast says so." She hoped it would. Some rainy days she liked to drive the car up to the top of Spinners Hill and sit in the little layby by the hillfort and let the rain drum on the roof. Some days she wanted to get out of the car and let the rain drum through her. Perhaps today was that day.

"Penny for them?" He looked at her with kind enquiry. There was never a real slur to Henry's voice. He masked it well, it was more a kind of thickness to one or two words, more if you caught him later in the day. She didn't really know how old Henry was. His hair was dyed to a deep coffee brown. He also dyed his eyebrows although there had been one memorable occasion last year when he appeared to have dyed only the left eyebrow. If she was being a police officer, she would hazard a guess that Henry was in his mid seventies. He was lean and tall in an undernourished way. Her mother called him 'rangy' which made Bryony think of panthers or the Kipling tiger, Shere Khan.

"I was just wondering about the rain. The forecast isn't always right." She smiled. "Although I like the rain."

"I like the rain if I have an umbrella. Or perhaps a window through which I can look out." Henry grinned.

"What are you up to?" Bryony asked with a nod to the secateurs in his hand.

"I'm barbering this. Been away of course and Mrs Farley next door has been dropping subtle hints about the state of the garden. Thought I'd better shake a leg." He pulled a grimacing face looking like an elderly and rather naughty schoolboy.

"I can mow the lawns for you if you like, when you're away." Bryony offered. Henry looked shocked.

"Oh my dear, I would never ask such a favour." He smiled "So I'm very glad you've offered." And he broke out into a smoky laugh. "We should seal the deal. Come in…come in for some coffee. If you have time?"

Bryony had been in Henry's cottage a few times only. He was not a full time resident, only showing up out of the blue two or three times a year. He might stay for a few months and then disappear again for another few. As a consequence the cottage had a frowsty scent to it, masked in some part by the rich aroma of Henry's cigars. Once in the kitchen she was not sure she wanted a drink. There was the remains of an Indian takeaway which was leeching turmeric onto the wooden table beside an emptied vodka bottle. A cat was licking some old coffee out of a china mug. Henry shooed the cat, tipped the contents of the mug into the sink and placed it ready by the coffee machine. It was a fancy state of the art gadget.

"So now I've lured you in here I can get straight to the point." Henry said, his face losing some of the bright and easy charm. "You know I've been away?" he asked. Bryony nodded.

"Of course. You watch all the houses. Our very own supercharged Neighbourhood Watch. Anyway, long story very short, Mrs Fartley next door…" he made the 'F' sound very hard, his thumb jagging to the party wall of the cottage, Bryony noted the nickname too and would have to be careful not to accidentally use it herself. "Old Fartley knocks on the door this morning and gives me a lecture about how my property is an eyesore and a security risk. Some bloody burglar will notice that the garden's a bit unruly and before we know it someone will 'cuckoo' the house." Henry held his hands out in confusion and wonder. "I mean…what the heck does the old bird mean? Cuckoo?" he filled the cat mug with coffee and placed it in front of Bryony.

Bryony felt a familiar shudder go through her. She drew herself up. She was in uniform. She was on her beat. She must step up.

"Cuckoo. It's a term they use when a drug dealer finds a house they can run drugs out of." She had managed to say it.

"What? Like when they grow cannabis? Balderdash. I'd like to see them try, you can't grow a spider plant in this place. All the low ceilings. Only thing that grows is moss and mushrooms." He gave a laugh. He was rather like an old school English film star, a kind of rougher David Farrar or Dirk Bogarde. He had that air about him. Bryony turned the mug to the side that she had not seen the cat lick and took a sip.

"Mm. No. No." it was excellent coffee. "No. Not growing the stuff." She felt braver "They'd do that in your shed probably. Cause you have electricity and water down there and that shed has that corrugated plastic roof and it gets hot in the summer."

Henry gave a gasp.

"Oh, lord, yes. That poor tabby last April." Henry shook his head, biting his lip with a mournful air. "So so dreadful. How it got in I will never know. What a disaster."

"Yes." Bryony recalled removing the half cooked remains and breaking the news to the tearful owner Mrs Justice, who lived two doors down.

"Didn't you have to bury it?" Henry's face registered anguish.

"I did. With full military honours…Anyway, the cuckooing is when they move into an empty house or the house of someone vulnerable, say one of their customers who is a bit of a wreckhead or vulnerable in some other way; owes them money or…that sort of situation. They take advantage, move in, make it their headquarters." Henry looked astonished. He thought about this information for quite a while, long enough that Bryony felt she had to sip a little more coffee.

"I take back all I said about the old cow. No wonder she was so agitated. Fuck. Ha. I'd like to see them cuckoo this place." Henry's face assumed, once more, the grim expression that had flashed across it when she had surprised him in the garden. She thought she liked Henry but the look on his face was unnerving. It was like a tiny shard of glass glinting out from his general charm.

"You were stabbed by a drug dealer, were you not?" Henry's charm burned diamond bright "That was what I heard."

"I don't know who stabbed me." She could expel the words, get them out, the words did not hurt. "I don't remember anything."

Henry nodded. She raised her mug of coffee, glad that her hand was not shaking too much. Henry leaned forward, his own mug gave off a waft of whisky as he chinked it with hers.

"Here's a toast to you, brave girl."

27

Badger

2019

The golf club turned in the air before coming to land with a thump on a patch of rough ten feet further on.
"It's a club not a spear." Fox was deadpan. He wasn't certain how the joke would land. His friend Mick Quinn was in a delicate mood this morning. It took a moment, a breeze heralding possible rain blew across them both and Mick laughed at last. He folded over, chortling, his hands resting on his knees.
"We are so unbelievably shit at this game." Mick's laugh was gathering momentum. Fox remained deadpan.
"And I was going to suggest we try for the Open."
Mick, still bent forward, began to hiss with mirth. He was shaking with it.
"I mean, I've only got one eye so I've no depth of field. But what's your excuse?" his chest was aching with laughter. "Why do we keep persisting?" he asked, the question punctuated with gasping mirth. Fox shrugged.
"Practice makes perfect?"
It was some moments before either of them could gather themselves enough to follow the club and the long lost ball. Behind them more serious players looked on in dismay. Umbrellas were being unfolded as the rain came on.
"It's worth it just to piss them off." Mick said. Fox agreed with a nod. "Also for access to that Tournedos Rossini stuff in the restaurant."
There were some more moments as they drooled a little at the thought of the steak dish and both took their shot for the green. The balls rolled and caromed around as if

stuffed with magnets that were polar opposites to the hole. As they attempted to putt the balls made a 2D orrery of little trails in the now rain soaked grass.

"I paid a call to that pawnbroker you suggested." Mick said when they were safely out of anyone's earshot in the woodland by the fifteenth hole. Even though they both used fluorescent neon balls they were unlikely to retrieve them from the bracken and brambles. "She was very helpful."
Fox nodded.

"Morag is a star." He said. Mick was swiping at the undergrowth. He seemed suddenly on edge.

"Is it right? Do you think?"
Fox frowned.

"Is what right?"
Mick stopped swishing and leaned on the club. It was slightly bent from its javelin type adventures.

"Me. Cashing that in." he looked troubled. Fox looked at him, his eyes narrowing. "D'you think it might be some sort of trick?"

"No. I don't. Whoever sent it to you sent it for a reason. That reason being that they took your eye. And your wife. And your job."
Mick drew himself up and was about to speak. Fox held up his hand to silence him.

"They took your eye. The bank lost a pile of over-priced and over prized yellow metal and received a fat cheque from the insurance company. An obese…a morbidly obese cheque."
Mick was about to interrupt once more but Fox held his hand straighter and more defiant.

"You received a compensation cheque so skinny it made Slimmer of the Year at Weight Watchers. You received a settlement so parsimonious and penny pinching that it broke Law Society records for the least amount awarded by a compensation panel ever."
Mick was shaking his head.

"Don't shake your head. Your eyepatch might fall off." Fox quipped. It burst the intensity of the exchange. Mick gave a weak smile.

"I've had a terrible week. I don't know. I thought it was the gold, that it had brought it all up. Been dreaming about the robbery. Don't know how many times I've walked down that corridor in the Radcliffe in my sleep this last seventy two hours."

Fox was sympathetic.

"It's not the gold. Or maybe it is. More likely it's the anniversary coming up." He reasoned. Mick groaned.

"Don't bloody remind me. The Chronicle are already after me. I had a journo this week asking me questions that…" he stopped speaking. He was visibly moved. He took in a shallow breath.

"What questions?" Fox was puzzled "About the anniversary? About how you feel? Personal stuff?"

Mick shook his head.

"I kid you not, this bloke was talking like I was in on it. He was asking stuff as if he was trying to trip me up. As if I was part of the crew." Mick's voice cracked a little. "Who thinks like that? If he could see the memory. If he could be right in that moment and I'm in that moment a lot. A lot, lately."

There was a moment of stillness between them, Mick calming himself, Fox in silent sympathy.

"Mate." Was all he could say, but it was enough. Mick picked up a little.

"I'll be ok. It's just…it's like you said. Twenty years. Twenty."

Fox nodded.

"Anyway. I've got this new therapist I'm supposed to see. She's going to do some kind of BDSM therapy or something? It's supposed to be great for trauma and PTSD." Mick could not understand why Fox was laughing. "What's so funny? BDSM. I was told that's what it was."

Fox almost choked.

"I think you mean EMDR mate. BDSM is what Tugger Matthews pays for at the Cavendish club."
It was Mick's turn to remain deadpan.

"Hey, you have the therapy you need. I'll have the therapy I need."

"You can have a loan of my handcuffs." Fox teased.

28

A Dink and a Prang

2019

Bryony had her notebook out and, to assuage Mr Justice's doubts she also took photos of the damage with her phone.

"Look…this dink here and…round this side…how did he even manage it? This prang. That's a proper prang, and look the bumper is ravaged." Mr Justice ran his fingers over the abrasions in the bumper of his Citroen. Just above that there was a dent in the rear wing which had taken off a gouge of paint.

"And even if he says he didn't do it I can guarantee there will be paint on his car. You can't make a prang like that and not have transference. Mark my words."

Bryony chatted for a while longer, taking details and making certain that Mr Justice felt calmer and more reassured than when she had been called to the scene of this crime.

"I will have a word with him Mr Justice." Bryony promised.

"When?" Mr Justice was angry. Bryony sympathised. She looked down the row of cottages and the parked vehicles. Henry's car was nowhere to be seen.

"His car isn't around." She mentioned the fact and pointed so that there could be no misunderstanding. "What I can do is pay him a call when he arrives home and let him know the situation."

Mr Justice considered and nodded agreement. He calmed visibly.

"Yes. Yes. Of course. No point going round if the old bastard isn't there." he turned to walk back in through his gate. "You are always as good as your word,

Bryony. Right. Thank you." And with a curt farewell wave he headed back indoors.

It was after five when Bryony returned from her patrol of the lanes and byways. She had spent some time at Hollow Tree Farm investigating a theft at one of the outbuildings. It was in the process of being turned into holiday accommodation and someone had come along and helped themselves to some slate slabs that were to make a patio.

She was rolling into the village and was aware of activity in the rear garden of one of the cottages on The Rows. It was clear that Rob Golightly was bedding in some slates on the top rank of his terraced garden. There was a small summerhouse, newly erected. She looked out for a parking spot and noticed Henry's car parked, somewhat erratically in the lane at the end of the street. She pulled in behind it. There were indeed the tell tale gouts of paint on the rear bumper where Henry's car had collided with his neighbours. The slates would wait.

She knocked at the door and although Henry did not answer there was the ghost of movement in the front room. A shadow passed across the mirror that looked out from the far wall. It occurred to Bryony that that mirror was placed exactly so that you could look out and see who was standing on the doorstep without being seen yourself. She tried slapping at the letterbox, the brass making a hollow dinging sound that could not be misheard. As she did so she saw the shadowed movement in the front room mirror once more. It had been an odd day and Bryony wanted to go home. Slates and pranged cars niggled at her. She gave a deep, weary sigh and stepped off the path to tap at the window. She was brazen and looked in, shielding her eyes with her hands to take the late afternoon glare off.

"Henry…you in? It's Bryony."
The door whipped open and Henry stood there. He looked greasy with drink which might account for the

erratic manner of his parking. His face bore the harsh look that disintegrated his charm.

"Fuck's sake what do you want? This isn't a village, it's an open prison." His mouth was spitty, his eyes glazed and wild and he stood back from the step. "What is it? For fuck's sake come in."

Henry had gone through to the kitchen and Bryony followed. Unconsciously she had hooked her fingers around the edge of her vis vest, feeling the edge of her body armour beneath.

"I'm sorry." Henry seemed to recover himself. He wiped a nervous hand over his face and then through his hair so that the sweat slicked it back. "I've had a trying day…week even. I'm sorry. What can I do for you Bryony?"

Bryony felt a choke of panic in her throat and she needed to breathe in, deeply.

"Mr Justice reported damage to his car this morning. He says you came home late and pranged the car. There's damage to the…"

Henry was nodding, he held up his hand.

"Please. Say no more…Let me get my cheque book." He turned to the sideboard drawer and took out a leather cheque book case and an old fashioned and expensive gold pen. "I meant to go and see him this afternoon but I was…waylaid by other matters. Do you think you could pop it in to him for me? Would that be an imposition?"

Bryony shook her head.

"Not at all. I have time to take it round."

Bryony watched him write the cheque, his signature a flourish. He tore the slip out and handed it over.

"Once again, dear girl, I'm sorry for my lack of manners just now. It really has been a trying time. No excuse but…"

Bryony shook her head and took a step towards the hall.

"Don't worry about it Henry. We all have those

days." He was moving round the table to see her out. She held up a hand, authoritative. "That's fine. I'll see myself out."

As she walked along the street to the Justice's cottage she looked at the cheque. It was drawn on a fancy private bank and she noticed that Henry's official name was B H Hallam. His signature was beautiful, very old school, not like her own scribble. She wondered what Henry's real first name was, must be something horrendous if he chose to use his middle name instead. Barnabas. Benedict. Beowulf. She imagined names as she walked down the path at the Justices' home.

At Rob Golightly's place she managed to comment on the garden from the neutral territory of Old Lane. It was clear from the moment she looked over the hedge that the slates were different. These had been carved with celtic designs by an artist in Pembrokeshire.

"Cost an arm and a leg but hey…" Rob looked at his handiwork. The slates made a twisting path from the summerhouse to the wooden steps down to the next bit of the terracing.

Bryony walked the length of Old Lane to blow the sticky cobwebs from her mind before heading home.

It was almost ten when she got the call.

"Bryony? Got a minute to come and rescue your dad?" it was Geoff at the Red Lion.

"He's not my dad Geoff." Bryony had told him this every time she'd rescued Henry.

"Well, whatever, the old gimmer needs an escort home. Soon as, 'cause he's getting gobby."

She walked down through the village. This errand of mercy would not take long and her mother was making them some supper in the meantime.

Geoff in the pub was relieved to see her come through the door. Henry was declaiming to Mr Justice but also the room in general.

"But WHERE has it gone? Hm? I ask you...I DEMAND to know where the community spirit is? I'll tell you, it has been EXORCISED by the forces of ...of modernity. By free trade. Where is the sense of camaraderie? Do you know?"

Mr Justice confessed that he didn't know and agreed with Henry.

"There's a slide, an inexorable slithering hellwards..." Henry's words were thickened with whisky and Bryony stepped up as he began making odd gestures, wiggling his hand downwards as if to illustrate the general decline.

"Hey Henry." She was bright and cheery and could feel the general sigh of relief from the pub's punters. "I thought you might walk me home." And she took his arm. He looked shocked for a moment and she thought she might have played it wrong, that Henry might turn on her. Instead he looked puzzled, recognised her and her arm and was in gentleman mode at once. He patted her arm, raised her other hand to his lips to kiss it with a wet, whisky kiss.

Out in the night air Henry took deep breaths.

"Oh. Oh." He stopped by the post box "I shall never tire of the breath of the country. I took so many wrong turnings my dear, so very many. A labyrinthine twisting..." his body was squirming away from her to reinforce this. "Byron, my father used to say, Byron you will go to the bad. Go to hell. And he wasn't wrong but oh, the fires burn bright and...my brother Tennyson. Oh. What a prig he turned out to be. Him and my father, prigs together. Stuffed into their shirts." He began to laugh a throaty, smoky chuckle that built into a hacking cigar cough.

It was as she saw him inside, in the light from the pendant bulb, that she realised that his hair had a line of white at the roots, that his teeth looked as if he hadn't cleaned them in some while. The veneer of charm had been peeled back in the wash of whisky. She felt a pang of sorrow and made him coffee.

It was two days later when Greg Hollins approached her to say that his car had been dinked by Henry in the middle of the night.

"Not left any insurance details or anything." Greg said "You've got to do something about him."

But nothing could be done. He did not return for several days and Bryony surmised that he had probably gone off on one of his jaunts elsewhere, in which case it would have to wait.

29

Venture Capital

2011

Kittredge. He was one of the least liked of the crew. It would be hard to find anyone he had ever worked with who liked him. But it wasn't a popularity contest.

The Midas Killing was like a big 'You Are Here' sign over the stupid bastard's head. The way Kittredge razed the little garden centre was breathtaking. It was a textbook role model for capitalism. Take something that people liked but that didn't make much profit and put a monster in its place. The little shed had been cutesy and welcoming. Mugs instead of cups. And what was the thing about hot tubs? A bath outside. Hadn't his Nan done that in the war? It was laughable.

As for Cordale Hall, there were some who said that place was cursed. That the original owner Sir Roger March had left it scarred by his villainy; orgies and wild parties, opium and gin. The original good time guy in fact. He doubted very much whether Kittredge's solicitor had brought that up in the property search.

And there was the walled garden, filled with an array of foxgloves, of hellebore, henbane and monk's hood. The original Poison Garden.

30

Cruickshank & Co Crew

Aromatherapy
2011

James Kittredge opened his sock drawer and let the LED lighting within illuminate the gold bar that nestled there. It rested on a specially formed nook lined with black silk velvet and he had to lift out the top layer, a honeycomb tray filled with his cashmere socks, to reveal it in all its beauty.

The smelting project he had initiated after Cruickshank & Co had been a bit of a disaster. His contact, Dicky Sly had proved exactly that. The small shed at the back of Dicky's property had set alight when they fired up the crucible. Emergency services had been called and it was only a day later that Kittredge realised he'd been had. It was quite a job to hunt down Dicky Sly and retrieve some of the bars they had been smelting. It was a lesson. To Sly certainly. That encounter had made the local papers as the Midas killing, Dicky Sly's face plastered in gold. Some might say that it was a waste but not Kittredge. It was a message. No one would ever mess with him again.

Kittredge had stashed the remainder in a self-storage unit, but kept this one bar in sight as a talisman. It was a thing of beauty this, ingot. He preferred the word 'ingot' but felt they were probably smaller. This was a proper fuck off slab of the glittery stuff. The surface of it appeared to hold light as if it was shining out from within. Here in the sock drawer it appeared lustrous. Elemental.

The word nibbled at his ear as he stroked the bar with more tenderness than he had ever shown any woman.

Aka Goldiggers. That was the label he kept sticky in his mental pocket and prided himself on his ability to spot the offenders. There was a certain type of strappy high heel that the bandits wore. This was usually teamed with enough make up for a small circus of clowns. Don't misunderstand, Kittredge loved Gold Diggers. He chose only of their herd, they were his preferred prey.

Take Poppy Gardiner, owner, or rather former owner of Poppy's Plot a local garden centre. For a start, what a ridiculous name for someone who was a gardener. Secondly. She had been a slightly different class of gold digger. She had smelt faintly of chicken shit and wood chip mulch and wanted a business investment rather than a handbag or a pair of Louboutins. Ordinarily he would not have given her the time of day but a friend of a friend at the golf club had shared a rumour that she was going down the pan and Kittredge saw an opportunity.

He'd scouted out the business and Poppy herself whose hair looked like it had been done in a hedge backwards as his Nana might say. He'd gone along on a spying mission with one of his 9carat gold diggers on a promise of lunch.

"It's a shed." Crystal had complained. He noted the Compeed blister plaster on her heel where her Louboutins rubbed.

"It's rustic and artisanal." He'd barked "Do you want a free lunch or do you want to sit in the car?"
He had got the measure of the place and then he'd visited his old mate Si at the accountants to get some in depth information.

His offer was the lowest he dared because he knew Poppy had little choice. She was going to lose her house inside six months if she didn't sell up. And of course his other mate at the estate agency helped a little with massaging the valuation. He was on fire with it. For the new garden centre Diggers, the third he had opened in the last five years, he had demolished the old shed and built a scorched larch lodge with bi-fold doors and a deck patio. The new restaurant had had a feature in Hallforth Life. The centre had more hot tubs than it had plants and it was becoming a destination lunch spot for some of the designer type 24 carat trophy wives.

Had Polly Poppy been pleased? Had she been grateful that his great dollops of cash had saved her house? No. She had been sick as a pig that she hadn't done the same. Not that she would admit it. Instead she had called him a flint hearted swindler to his face. A swindler? What was she? Victorian?

He had met Lindy at a 'Business Breakfast' held in a marquee at an otherwise woeful local Enterprise Week. Kittredge had a lot of connections in the local business community, men in suits who employed local people and played a lot of golf. He avoided their 'games nights' which involved poker and the loss of quantities of cash. Take a long look at Wilkinson folks, the biggest loser of all time if gossip was to be believed. He had, at the last inventory, the suit he stood up in and was possibly sleeping in his car.

Lindy had caught his eye because she looked to him like a 24 carat Gold digger, his favourite kind, and she owned The Amaranthus Spa at Cordale Hall. This enterprise was very classy and occupied the east wing including the conservatory and the walled garden. He was currently very keen on acquiring a stake in this business and since Lindy was currently looking for outside investment it seemed the perfect match.

He'd come along to an initial meet at Cordale Hall. While he was impressed by her set up he felt Lindy was a bit up herself. While he was there he took the opportunity to take a look around the rest of the Hall. It was a grand old residence divided into a boutique hotel in the North and South Wings and the West was exclusive private apartments.

After this brief history he was not then best pleased to rock up at Cordale Hall for his third and, he hoped, conclusive meeting with Lindy to find her chatting with Polly Poppy in the walled garden. He parked the car and, gritting his teeth, made his way along the gravel path to the small pergola where they were holding their powwow.

"Can we make a start?" he flicked his wrist out with its golden watch, a piece hand tooled for him in Birmingham's jewellery quarter by a goldsmith he knew. It was a unique piece. He had toyed with the idea of having Cruickshank & Co written on the face like a brand name but he reined himself in at the last minute.

"Hello Mr Kittredge." Lindy said with her best service industry smile.

"Hello." Polly Poppy said. At least she'd brushed her hair. She was sipping at a mug of coffee.

"Don't you have something to mow?" Kittredge had no time for her. Lazing about.

"Well I did have a garden centre 'til someone stole it." Polly Poppy said. He glanced at the table unwilling to dignify that remark with a response. There was some artwork visible and a laptop.

"Poppy is my new garden designer." Lindy said. He had wanted to come in like a heat seeking missile or a Bond villain. Polly Poppy was just cluttering the place up.

"Is it your garden to design?" he gave her a knowing and sarcastic look. "I think you'll find that the walled garden is the property of the Cordale Hall group." He gave a self satisfied smile.

"She's designing the garden at my house." Lindy was not cheery or in a negotiating mood. "Anyway Mr Kittredge I'm glad that you've arrived early. I don't want to delay you any further…"

"I've instructed my legal team to draw up a draft agreement. You won't have to worry about any transitional phase." He was pulling out his phone.

"I'm sorry, I think you've raced a little ahead of yourself. I wanted to tell you today that I have found investment elsewhere." Lindy looked stoic.

"Investment?" he was struggling with his poker face. Actually this turned out even better with Polly Poppy as a witness. He had been unsure how this whole conversation might go, now it appeared to have diverted onto his tracks.

"Yes. I appreciate all the effort and the consultations we've had in the last couple of weeks but... I've decided that won't be taking up your investment option after all."

Kittredge looked at her. The morning was suddenly sunshine and roses.

"Didn't I mention? It isn't an option." he was relishing this "I was coming today to withdraw my investment offer."

Lindy looked relieved. Polly Poppy looked suspicious. He was slightly worried about the coffee mug, it was a hefty handthrown number. Handthrown being the key wording.

"Oh. Well that's something of a relief. I was worried that..." Lindy was smiling. Wipe that off.

"I have also decided on a different route. The agreement my legal team have drawn up is between you and I as Landlord and tenant. It will supercede your current agreement."

It was Lindy's turn to frown.

"What?"

"I have already made an investment, in Cordale Hall."

Kittredge saw her heart sink down into her shoes. It was a crowning moment of his life. Pause for effect, take in a

breath. Now.
"I bought it."

One of the perks of being Lord of Cordale Hall was that he could use the spa as often as he liked.
"You have to stop this right now or I will call the police." Lindy's office was not as tidy as he had expected.
"Our agreement was that I could use the spa and have whatever facilities I required."
Lindy stood her ground.
"You cannot sexually harass my staff. I will not stand for it." Her face had gone a bright prawny pink even under the layer of foundation. Was she perhaps contemplating him sexually harassing her? He wanted to make a joke about customer service but the words wouldn't fall into the right place. He remained silent but with a broad smile on his face. This was not the time for jokes, this was the time for the big stick.
"I have the power of God over you and your business." He spoke quietly, he felt masterful. "I can put your rent up. I can throw you out." He snapped his fingers. "I can tell the police you are running a brothel and ruin you."
He had never been as shocked as he was when he snapped his fingers for the final time and Lindy broke down in tears.
He was so stressed by this experience that he headed to the bar for a restorative brandy before walking to the front desk to book himself a 'full' spa treatment.
"Full." He emphasised the word to the young woman on the desk " 'Full' spa treatment. I want that little blonde one. Dina?"
"Dana." Lindy came through from the office "Dana is on leave today." He saw the look the first girl gave her so he knew that was a lie. "You will be in room 3. I will send someone through."

He was most put out to be lying bollock naked on the massage table with a creditable semi-on and find out that he had been sent Guy the masseuse. It was like being rugby tackled.

"Want a happy ending?" the lad asked at the end, his face entirely serious. Kittredge scrabbled into his bathrobe. "Thought not, you bastard."
There was something wrong with the massage too, his skin was burning.

"That'll be the chilli oil. Enjoy your tea." And the young man left.

The tea was not served by the usual little catering girl. Instead the tray had been left by the seating outside the cold plunge. He lifted the little cast iron pot and filled the Japanese beaker beside it. There was no one around to wait on him. He sipped at the tea which tasted a little off because it had been left sitting in the pot for god knew how long. With no one to bully, harass or complain to, he knocked the rest of the beaker back and headed into the sauna.

He had not been in there very long before he started to feel a little odd. His heart was fluttering about and a wave of nausea was rising. A figure loomed out of the steam and tipped the ladle onto the rocks. More steam furled and he tipped the ladle once again. Kittredge felt the heat of it catch in his throat, he could barely breathe. Who was that? The figure reached for the ladle and instead of tipping it over the stones he hit Kittredge in the chest. Bop. Bop. Bop. Kittredge felt his heart racing like a greyhound. He couldn't breathe, he must get out...he must...his feet skidded from under him, or did the figure trip him? He was burning, burning with chilli oil, burning with the hot rocks now as he fell forward onto the little brazier and his heart raced on. Catching up to the rabbit, catching up now, out of breath. The end of the race and who was that? Was that Polly Poppy? Was that Lindy?

Crystal? It could not be Ivo Regan. It could be as his heart reached the finish line and all the faces of anyone he'd ever met paraded past his closing eyes and the clouds of steam in the sauna became something like the clouds of Heaven. Except that a figure loomed out of them one final time and he was The Devil.

31

He Who Laughs Last

2019

Owen King stood on his terrace at Jericho House and surveyed his kingdom. He would scrag that gardener for the way he'd pruned that apple tree but other than that the outlook was nothing short of an epic vista.

He was the most successful businessman in, probably, the four or five nearest counties. He, Owen King, former rapscallion and bit of a lad, was the longest serving councillor for East Hill. He was going to be Mayor. He was Mr Charity Gala himself, always popping up on the local news planting trees for this and handing out cash for that. The local Knights gathered at his Round Table. Over the years, twenty years, he had donated several important artworks to the Radcliffe Collection. He'd endowed an art prize named for his wife, The Alexandra Prize. He was Chair of the Radcliffe Collection Board. His portrait, commissioned by local artist Romilly Carew, was going to hang in the Grand Hall.

As he stood on the terrace pumped up on his own kudos, he spared a thought for PC Whiteleg. This old git of a police officer had hounded his every footstep as a boy. You couldn't nick a yoyo from Sam Taylor's Toy Emporium without old PC Whiteleg giving you the run around and making you give it back. He made you eat the sweets you'd pinched from the Pick n Mix until you were sick and then he'd make you wash the sick off his boots. His lean and hungry face with its brush of a moustache had popped up in the wing mirror or rear view of every car he'd tried to nick as a teenager. PC Whiteleg was about setting examples, he was about role modelling and giving people a chance to do good. He didn't want to arrest anyone and have a foolish childhood prank ruin their life. He believed in community policing. He believed in that right up until the moment Owen King ran him over in a stolen VW Golf in 1988.

Owen had torched it of course, the blaze destroying all evidence and becoming, for Owen at least, a beacon of proof that you could get away with murder. Didn't see any portraits of PC Whiteleg hanging in the Radcliffe did you? Owen King grinned and raised his tumbler of whisky in a toast to his long dead nemesis. He hoped the old bastard's ghost was there at his inauguration as Mayor.

There was a lot of kerfuffle surrounding the appointment as Mayor. All the bigwigs were brushing off their evening jackets. He had been delighted at how easy it was for him to suggest that the event take place on the 30th August. It was triumphal, to have this black tie civic event in his honour, to unveil his portrait in the Radcliffe collection on the twentieth anniversary of the Cruickshank & Co robbery. Hey, PC Whiteleg, who laughs last, eh? He was enjoying this moment when the terrace doors opened behind him. He turned.

"What do you want?" he was less than pleased. Ivo Regan had seemed like his lieutenant at one point, a Mercutio to his Romeo. Perhaps. At the moment he was uncertain about the younger man.

"We need to talk."

"Nothing to talk about. You know where we are. You know what needs doing." Owen was shutting him down. He was not having Ivo Regan of all people call the agenda. He did not need this kind of irritant at such a crucial moment in his illustrious career.

"This is the endgame Owen." Ivo toyed with his cufflinks.

"Endgame is it? Didn't have you pegged for a chess buff." Did the lad think he could overstep his mark? It struck him that Ivo was now in his forties. What was he? Forty two or three? Alexandra would know. He was the lad no longer, Owen thought of something Alexandra had said, something Shakespearean.

"It's time Owen. We must talk this out. It is time." Ivo was steely. What did he mean? Time for a coup?

Owen King had only to reference his own young ambition to be set on edge. Alexandra's words came back to him now, was he certain, she had asked, if Ivo was Macduff or Iago? Ivo did a good job at the Casino which served as a front for many of Owen King's more lucrative and less legal pursuits. His heir apparent, that was how he had regarded the young man. But there was something off kilter about him of late. He was getting above himself. Owen was watchful. This whole black tie thing, this apex of his achievement would be the perfect backdrop for a hostile takeover. Et tu Ivo?

"You can't say anything I don't already know." Owen bluffed. He gave the young man a hard and authoritative stare. Ivo nodded and seemed to breathe out.

"So how is this going to play out?" he asked. Owen fought the urge to lash out. He was wired now, not at all the mood he wanted.

"It plays out when it plays out. Why haven't you found Henry?" that was the way, slap him down. Owen had pushed of late for that last piece of their puzzle. Ivo drew himself up again. Cocky instead of chastised.

"I've found Henry." No. There it was again, that little edge sparking off him. He made Owen nervous these days. Get rid of him. Soon as.

"Then why are you here? Is Henry here?" Owen King looked around with a theatrical gesture "Do what you have to do Ivo."

And Ivo Regan was dismissed.

32

End Game

2019

The thing about chess was the language of it. Gambit. Castling. Rook. It was the medieval, the ancient, the unchanging power struggle of humanity. For him it had also been the carving of the pieces of the set he had played with his father. Even now he kept an eye out for it in junk shops and vintage emporiums. A treasure hunt of a different kind. White on the right. Queen on her own colour.

Was that where he was? His task almost done. Ah yes, the final pieces. Who remained? The King. Rook. Bishop. Pawn.

Never underestimate the power of the Pawn. His father put the piece down before the King on the remembered board. Threat and sacrifice.

Endgame.

33

A Matter of Time

2019

'*Fairview*' Henry's caravan had, with some cladding, perfected the disguise of a log cabin. All the other cabins, on the small and remote park, had Welsh names, a cacophony of consonants so unrecognisable to him that Henry felt he could be in Japan or Russia. His own small dwelling was burrowed into the dunes on the coastal side. To the rear his wooden deck sat in the lee of the dunes giving a private and secretive view out to sea. This was his bolthole, the place he retreated to when pushed. And of late he felt pushed.

He felt so pushed that as he drove in through the wooden gates, he was scanning the park for untoward signs. The only other people he had encountered that week were the couple from the caravan at the very top of the park. '*Carreg Cennen*' had a wraparound deck and two stately stone hounds stood watch at the door. They had been packing up their tank of a car this morning as he brewed his coffee. He did a drive by to make certain that they were gone. Yes. He had the park to himself. It was past four and so the girl on reception had already locked up and her little runabout was gone. There was no movement anywhere. Blinds were drawn. Shutters were down. Bliss. He rolled along the road towards his own miniature haven.

Earlier that day when he had been in town, the nearest being very small and far away, the weather had been bright hot summer sunshine. As he flirted with the waitress on the terrace at the gallery café he had felt his hair melting to his head like liquorice. This was Pembrokeshire however and now, in late afternoon, the sky was something like Payne's Grey, a Turneresque sky.

As he stepped out of the car a heavy thermal blew across him, rattling at '*Fairview*' and its wooden cladding, heralding the imminent arrival of a thunderstorm.

He had picked up some groceries at the farm shop and now his artisan sourdough bread had blown off the top of the box and under the lodge steps. He wedged the door open with the box and stepped back down. He felt the muscle in his back give a warning twinge but, hey ho, bread rescued. He picked up the box of goodies and shouldered his way in. There was a bottle of Brecon gin to be savoured with some of the bread and the Teifi Celtic Promise cheese. Life was about the little treats.

"Hello Henry."

The gin bottle bounced from Henry's startled hand and, mercifully unbroken, rolled towards Ivo Regan's feet. Ivo reached down to retrieve it.

"I knew it was only a matter of time." Henry's voice did not waver, even though his heart was going like a steam engine. "You have been a busy boy. With your To Do In list."

Henry's thrust with the breadknife was parried by the Brecon gin and he had to duck to avoid being concussed by it. The bottle, as Ivo swung it, carried on its trajectory and collided with the edge of the cupboard. It smashed. Ivo jabbed the broken glass but Henry snatched up a shard and tore at Ivo's face. Blood spurtled. Giving Henry just enough time to reach for the cricket bat hidden by the stove.

34

News Feed Frenzy

2019

The news story, in The Chronicle, had a sort of dirty kudos angle to it. The Cruickshank & Co crew, the ones that got away with it. They had acquired an almost Robin Hood status, enhanced by the fact that no one had ever been identified as a suspect. It was a measure of the depths of this journalism that the only photos in the article were of retired police officer Rory Fox and disabled former security officer Michael Quinn.

"No one calls me Michael." Mick said, as if this was the most important of the factual errors and random speculation that had been printed. "And I'm not disabled."

There had been a small news feeding frenzy. All the local radio stations had called for interviews which Mick refused to give. The angle of the story in The Chronicle was that Mick Quinn had been in on the whole job, that the loss of his eye was somehow a kind of twisted alibi.

Mick and Fox were watching the local tv news which was filling all its airtime with Mick's alleged sacrifice of his eye to the glory of crime. They had sandwiched footage of a reporter standing outside a house, not Mick's house as it turned out, in between stories of local councillor, Owen King planting a tree in the arboretum and future mayor and local councillor Owen King opening the new dogs home.

Mick had tried to speak to the journo at The Chronicle, Daniel Wellesley, in a bid to stop the story.

"Should have given me the interview." Was all the young man would say before hanging up.

"Wish I had given it to him. This is a circus."

Mick was tired. He had had trouble sleeping of late. The imminent twentieth anniversary of the robbery was triggering unwanted and long buried memories in spite of his recent sessions of EMDR therapy.

Fox was more cynical.

"He'd have done the same story and he'd have used the same photo and he's a little shit." Fox was disgusted. It seemed outrageous that an innocent man, a victim of a crime, should have to put up with this media treatment when the real villain was pictured grinning and wielding a shiny new spade at the Arboretum.

They had decided to go early to the golf course to hammer a few balls and shift the general mood of unease and despondency. It was working until the ninth hole with Fox poised to take his shot.

"Twenty years since the Cruickshank job eh? Twenty years and no resolution. Hey, Fox?...Are the Guinness Book of Records getting a look in?" Neil Jolly had introduced the subject of the news story and now thought he was the funny man. Fox ignored him. The group, made up of Neil and his chief cronies, Jack Still, Logan Howard and Hunter Hudson had caught them up. Fox had suggested they play round but they had declined on account of their true agenda.

"I said, Guinness Book of Records looking for 'Longest Case in Criminal History' d'you think?" Neil was shaking his head, making a tutting sound. His mates were smirking. Mick was looking at his muddied ball, sitting on the green.

"Not a clue." Neil was struggling but desperate. "Not one clue."

"It doesn't get any more relevant the more times you repeat it, Neil." Fox snatched up his ball and prepared to move on.

"Don't you ever think that when you're looking at your mate here, you might be looking at a clue?" There were sniggers from the group.

"Meaning?" Fox looked directly at Neil who had the good grace to quail just a little.

"Meaning…he was the security guard. Someone let the thieves in that day, someone had a key to the kitchen door." There was a murmur of smugness which passed through the group. It was Hunter Hudson, however, who caught the expression that settled on Fox's face and took a step back.

"Your cousin had a summer job at the Radcliffe that year. Holly Jolly?" the smirking stopped abruptly.

"My Holly?" Logan Howard was pale faced. Holly Jolly was now Holly Howard, his wife. "What's my Holly got to do with it?"

"That summer Holly Jolly was going out with Jex Lennox, who, at the time, was on a roster of possible prominent nominals for the Cruickshank job in the CID at City Central. There was a lead, quoshed by your uncle, that she gave the gang the key to the kitchen."
There was a harsh silence. Logan glared at Neil Jolly.

"What the fuck…who the fuck do you think you are Fox?" Neil was cornered "Isn't it obvious the security guard let them in? Fuck's sake you were probably in on it too. He let them in and then you didn't catch them. Where's your stash, Fox? Up your arse?"
There was no humour now, just the scent of a fight.

"And what about you? Hm?" Fox was the big gun now, unforgiving. "What about you hanging around with Owen King? Hm? King of the town and a crook however many suits he gets from his tailor. Just like the rest of the Council with their hands in someone's pocket. Where's the grant money for the new leisure centre Jack? Eh?"
Fox dodged the club, swung with professional aplomb by Jack Still. As Logan, Neil and Hunter restrained Jack, Mick was quick to grab Fox and bundle him into the nearby golf buggy. As they careered towards the eighteenth and the safety of the club a well played ball

pinged off the buggy roof. 850 yards from the ninth. No par.

Daniel Wellesley, journalist, was not having a great night. He had attempted to pay for the cosmically priced cocktails with his credit card and it had been declined. It had been declined three times.

"Try again." He whispered to the barkeep. The young woman shook her head.

"If you're not embarrassed, I am embarrassed for you." She handed him back his card. Daniel did not notice her name badge but she knew him. He had done something of a hatchet job on her mum's dog grooming business last year after a break in. Daniel could have offered her a bar of Cruickshank gold in payment and she would most likely have hit him with it. He was forced to ask his date if she could help.

The conversation had been frosty anyway. It was their first date, they'd met at a local political hustings, and she had been obsessed with talking about the Cruickshank anniversary story and she, oh God he couldn't think of her name, something beginning with J? Anyway she was an opinionated bitch.

"This man lost an eye you know. I don't think that is an alibi. He's a victim not a perpetrator." She was jabbing at the story in the newspaper which she had brought with her.

"It's the perfect alibi." Daniel persisted. She was a write off.

"Seriously, why would you write this? Is this 'journalism'?" she was even resorting to the air borne quotation marks. If he could just nip to the loos and ditch her he might be able to get to the Cavendish and salvage this sinking ship of an evening.

"I just need the…" he stood up. As he did so something gloopy and brown slammed into his eye from above and there were screams and the sound of glasses breaking.

Something beginning with J, who turned out to be Julia, ran him to the A&E where the stuff was sluiced out of his eyeball with considerable discomfort. His vision was blurred but he was assured the damage was not going to be permanent. The missile had irritated his cornea and that it would take a couple of days to recover.

"I've put on a pad but if you find that's uncomfortable then you can remove it and just wear dark glasses for a couple of days." The nurse was about to dismiss him. "Any problems just go and see your GP."

"It must have been an eagle or something." Daniel speculated. The nurse, filling in the last of her paperwork, paused to look at him.

"Sorry?" she was not very interested but he was feeling a bit shaken and the painkillers were taking effect.

"It must have been an eagle…that shat on me…to have fallen so heavily like that. To cause this damage." He pointed to his newly bandaged eye.

"Nah. That brown stuff wasn't bird shit. Unless eagles have started eating chilli powder. And, judging by the bruising around your socket, whatever it was hit you at some pressure, maybe from a catapult? Or a paintball gun? I see stuff like this sometimes from stag dos at the paintball place."

Daniel had a lot to think about. He had, somewhere in the evening, lost his phone and his wallet. The symbolism of being hit in the eye was also not lost on him. Not that he had anyone to talk this over with. On leaving A&E he realised that bolshy Julia had abandoned him and he would have to walk home.

35

Art for Art's Sake

Friday 30th August 2019

There had been champagne for breakfast to accompany scrambled eggs and smoked salmon. Owen made a silky scrambled egg.

"I like to cook for you." He said as Alexandra poured their coffee and he popped the toaster. They sat at the kitchen table. The kitchen was not the minimalist palace people might expect. Alexandra, as Owen put it, was a country girl at heart. None of the house had been torn out or remodelled. It had been restored under Alexandra's careful and tasteful eye. There were flags on the kitchen floor, uneven and original and making it necessary to shore up the far leg of the table with a coaster. It was an old table, elegant and in keeping with the period of the house. There were no silent close cupboards or space age taps and hobs. The Aga ticked with heat. The cleaner was not allowed in the kitchen proper. This was Alexandra's territory. Mrs Nolan had to use the utility room for her mid-morning cup of Earl Grey.

"You like to cook eggs." Alexandra laughed. "Your cook book would be very thin." Owen looked up from buttering the toast. She was ten years younger than him and sometimes he really felt it. He felt protective and yet she was a resourceful and capable woman. She was his lodestone.

They sat at the table.

"I put out your clothes for tonight." Alexandra usually chose his clothes. It wasn't that he couldn't be bothered, it was that he liked to wear what she had chosen. "I ordered you some more shirts when I was down at Dragorian's yesterday. In that linen you liked."

Owen ate with a silver fork from a china plate and he looked out of the tall kitchen window at the deer park beyond. His own deer park. He felt tears prickle at the thought of old PC Whiteleg and his relentless pursuit of the delinquent Owen. Where had PC Whiteleg lived? In the Lodge Park on the far side of the city. Where had Owen King ended up? His own deer park and neo-classical Jericho House, the crowning acreage of his extensive property portfolio. Christ, he even owned the Lodge Park.

"Are you alright?" Alexandra asked with amusement rather than concern "You've got a funny look on your face. As if you just won Miss World or something and want to thank everyone for world peace." Owen King reached for her hand. The rings on the fourth finger of her left hand were made from Cruickshank gold.

"I was just thinking. All this portrait stuff, being the Mayor…makes me reflect on things."

"It's a big event tonight. In your honour." Alexandra smiled "It's exciting. Do you think we can have private access to the Gallery at some point? I particularly mean the Cupola gallery at the very top. You know the one with the velvet sofas?" her eyes glimmered at him, her lips pursing in a way that he had no power over. "Do you think darling? Celebrate in style?" and that grin. My God he had never loved anything as much as he loved her.

"I'm not the self-made man they think I am." He said. Alexandra gave a snortle of laughter.

"No. Most of what you have you stole." She leaned in and stood up to clear the plates. He held her hand tight.

"I could not be me, without you."
She demurred with a kiss.

"Oh you did alright before me."
He was not to be dissuaded. He pulled her closer, intense

and emotional. There was a faint scent of horse about her, flesh and saddle. Intoxicating.
     "You are a class act." And she saw that he meant it.

Later, after they'd broken some of the china and Alexandra had scrambled egg stuck to her bare backside, Owen headed out for a round of golf.

It was a strange morning. Owen King rode about in his golf buggy as if he was that very thing; King of the city. Twenty years ago today he had been part way through the robbery of the century, he and his crew getting away with £30 million. As the other golf club members fawned over him and basked in his glory now that he was going to be Mayor, he thought of all the secrets folded into everyone. If they knew who he really was what would they do? Then he thought of the council meetings, of the backhanders and deals done, even at this local level, the greased and dirty cogs of this small city. He was feeling very philosophical. It must be a result of the sittings for the portrait. It had given him time to consider himself.

     Romilly had finished the portrait by the skin of her teeth. Only twenty four hours ago the movers had arrived with their van to take her masterpiece away. She had no doubt in her mind about this portrait. She had taken on portrait commissions before, the cash subbed her real painting, as she saw it. This portrait had been different from the get go.
     It was the scale of it, it was a good ten foot square. The moment she met him for preliminary sketches the scale screamed out at her. The frame was gilded, her colleague at Prisk and Son had done an excellent job. They had even found some old bits of frame to be repurposed, something that Romilly was

keen on. The sometimes mismatched pieces were placed into something new, led the eye on a journey if it cared to look, one that framed the work with a gravitas. It was locked within history.

It was also the personality of the man she had painted. She was in her sixties now, probably ten years or more older than him. She had never, in all her life, met anyone quite like him. He had a reputation, not just as a successful businessman in the city, there was the whispered reputation, that he was a crook, but then, you could say that about three quarters of the council. She did not understand what had gone on in her own studio. The Muse had parachuted in.

He had walked into the studio that first morning and he dragged with him a fierce, dark energy. Romilly had always had an open frequency for other people's energy. As a child she had avoided being bullied by firstly, being able to detect the bad energy and avoid it where possible. Secondly she had a knack of freaking out the perpetrators with her supernatural knowledge of how ugly and twisted and broken they were inside. It was, in fact, the chief reason her portraits were so popular. Her portraits had a life to them that was imbued through her ability to tap energy. No one was glossed over or beautified but she could use the paint to illustrate something specific in them, the light or darkness that made them who they were. It lent the portraits a mesmerising edge. It was a bit Dorian Grey really. If she was honest with herself it was part of the reason she didn't take on portraiture as her main outlet. It came from elsewhere, a little overgrown path of her creativity that scared her a little. She was kidding herself that they were inconsequential. In reality she had been hiding. She thought now that all those other portraits had been simply sketches, prepping her for this.

Owen King was only too glad to pose. On that first session he had wanted to brag about himself, and

Romilly had shut him down quickly. She did not want to listen to his hubris all day long. They had worked for three hours that first session and the silence she enforced had, she understood, given him respect for her. He had not been able to control this situation, or her. She was in charge, with her little palette knife and her pencils.

"I don't need to ask if I can see the sketching." He did not move from his place in the studio. He gave her a measured look.

"There's no point. It's just sketching. A working through of ideas. I think you need to be on a horse." Romilly had been inspired. She thought of his stables out at Breedon. "I'll need to come out to the stables. You can pick your favourite."

He had paused a moment and then nodded assent. He moved across the studio.

"I wasn't sure about you at first. I wanted David Knightley." He offered the information as if he thought she might be cowed. Romilly said nothing. For some time. Owen King knew when he was defeated.

"Now I'm here I think you're the best choice." He had decreed and offered a hand for her to shake. It felt like a bargain with the devil.

At the stables she met his wife, she sketched the horse Golden Boy. She was glad to get away. She returned to the studio and although she had intended only to make some sketches, rough up a few ideas, she worked in deadly earnest until the small hours.

There had been several sittings. As the days and weeks had gone on she felt more and more that this was her masterpiece but it was an uneasy feeling. Images came to her for the background and she thumbed through her art school copy of Hall's to track down the symbols she needed. She trawled the city taking photos of gargoyles and pilasters from across the civic buildings. The horse reared up in her imagination so that the portrait took on an element of Whistlejacket being ridden by Napoleon. She had never worked so hard and so intensely on anything in her life. It made her anxious. It felt as if it might never be finished.

And then it was. And here it was now being winched into place for the ceremony. She felt a little breathless about it, that sorrowful excitement of saying goodbye to something.

"Left a bit?" Imogen, the Radcliffe's curator was looking at her. Romilly had a sudden dread, had she left a bit? Was there something missing? Imogen reached a hand to Romilly's arm.

"Hey. You alright?" the crew on the gantry moved the portrait a centimetre or two to the left.

"Oh. Yes." Romilly felt a rush of relief, she patted Imogen's hand. "Yes. The wall is the perfect foil by the way. Which did we go for? Castle Stone was it or the Naiad Grey?" she looked at the portrait. The terrible man looked back at her. She felt a little bit sick, as if she was being given a message that she might never paint anything again, at least, nothing that was as magnificent.

"Milly, we could have hung this on bare brick love, it would still be the most magnificent portrait. You've outdone yourself." she turned to look at her, very direct "I could look at this all day everyday and see something else. It's a masterwork." She leaned in to hug Romilly and whispered.

"You painted his soul, Milly. Every dark corner of it. For whoever looks to see."

Preparations for the black tie red carpet unveiling were not going according to plan. For a start some idiot had sanctioned roadworks directly outside the Radcliffe Collection and there were diversions and tailbacks. Guests were being greeted at the end of the street by volunteers and walked along past the open trench and the temporary fencing to the steps at the entrance. Imogen was unruffled, everything was running late but it wasn't brain surgery, a portrait and champagne buffet could be delayed.

The local tv news crew were a pain so Imogen had put her assistant, Dora, in charge of them. Dora was also a pain so they were a perfect match. Late in the afternoon Imogen, with a well deserved mug of coffee in her hand, watched from her office window as the road crew toiled below. She felt the road roller as it made its lumbering progress. The scent of tarmac being poured was pungent. Where was that bloke going on the roller? On and on and on and where the hell? Oh. Round the back of the building. The floor was shaking, she hoped the vibrations weren't disrupting anything in the china gallery. She ought to check. She looked at her gown hanging on the coat rack. It was a vintage velvet number. Might be about time to squeeze her carcass into it.

She headed downstairs to the basement and the staff loo. Walking along the corridor she was reminded of the Cruickshank & Co robbery. There was a patch in the wall that had been concreted over but never painted. Twenty years ago today. She had been fourteen and already a regular at the Radcliffe.

She nearly broke the zip on the vintage velvet but, that disaster averted, a new one arose as she realised she'd forgotten her shoes.

Alexandra King knocked on her husband's dressing room door. She had not noticed the absence of sound from within.

"Owen...are you nearly..." his clothes that she had selected for him this morning were still where she had placed them. There was no sign of him. He must be in the shower after his golf.

He was not in the shower. He was not, in point of fact, in any of their showers.

"He left about four." This voice was decisive in

its vagueness. She had called all his golf mates and no one had a real idea but the barman at the club was reliable.

"About four?" Alexandra was feeling edgy. This event was a big deal. Owen could be filled with a little hubris at times and think he could keep everyone waiting because he was the King. Tonight's event would only confirm that notion in his head. He'd probably be unmanageable after all this. "When about four?"

"Five minutes past." The barman confirmed "I'd checked my watch because I was due my break." Owen King was not answering his phone. Alexandra, in her unease, had forgotten to put an earring in her left ear. She hurried to the car, waiting in the drive. She could not delay any longer. What was he up to? It was not beyond him to have some extra plan. He was, no doubt, going to make an entrance. She loved him very deeply but sometimes, she thought, as the car was diverted and she had to make her way along the street past the roadworks, she really just wanted to slap his cocky face.

     The Radcliffe Collection Grand Hall was filled with the self-styled great and the good of the city. All the councillors were there and the tailors and boutiques had raked in a lot of cash for gowns and suits. Well, more likely a lot of credit. All the guests were getting a little restive. They were already half an hour awry timing wise.

"Any joy?" Imogen Rust, the curator, was a model of composure. Alexandra wished she was as composed. She shook her head. Why wasn't he answering? Where was he? She had already sent Derek back in the car for him. She was furious. How dare he do this.

"I wouldn't worry. The roadworks have botched everything today. He's probably caught in traffic…"

"He was supposed to be with…" Alexandra

hushed herself. She did not want to panic. "You're right. He was coming from the golf club so…"

"I came from the golf club." Terry Aitchison was draining the last of his welcome champagne. Behind them there was a sudden cracking sound and a deep sighing, rushing sound as of heavy fabric crumpling earthward. A deep hush was followed by a scream that could etch glass. It was joined by a chorus of similar screams, like a choir in hell.

Seeing the curtain fall away, Imogen acted quickly, pushing Alexandra King behind a statue so that she could not see the terrible portrait now revealed.

Romilly's masterpiece, obscured by a frame made from fence posts dripped with what looked like molten gold. Within it, Owen King, flattened out like a paper doll.

"Is it a Damien Hirst?" asked Terry Aitchison.

36

Family Tree

2019

It had been lovely living with her mother, but Bryony Wolfe had found a cottage in the village at last. Her move had prompted some clearing out. If she was honest she felt like burning everything and starting again but that seemed a bit dramatic. She needed to be measured and calm.

She had the afternoon off and so far she'd chucked a few old clothes in a bin bag for the charity shop and was mooching over her bookcase. In the corner of the bottom shelf was an old keepsake box she'd had forever. It was a little like a black hole, things vanished into it that seemed to mean a great deal but, in reality, in the last year she hadn't bothered to even look inside. She didn't want to look back. She was afraid to look forward. She opened the box.

Half of the trinkets and gewgaws inside brought back no significant memory. There were some tickets for bus journeys that must, at some point in her history, have had significance but she was throwing them in another bin bag right now. This felt good. To have this box emptied and restart it. It was a lovely wooden box with a little key, Victorian, that her mother had given her. It ought to be out in sight. She could put jewellery in it. Or pens. Something useful so that she would look at it every day.

At the very bottom under a selection of broken beads was a much folded piece of paper. The second she saw it the memory prinked with a scent of school corridors and of the sunlight that day streaming through the curtains in the assembly hall. She had not looked at this in some time. The last occasion had been her

University graduation when she had carried it in her pocket, a talisman. It had found its way into the box after she had moved from her harbour flat in the city following her incident. What a useful word that was. Locking up all that had happened.

She unfolded it. The Cruickshank & Co crew family tree diagram. She could recall Fox's voice, his demeanour, the slightly pissed off air of Mr Daniels the games teacher. Dust motes in the air and some of the students in front of her craning to see what Fox was drawing on the whiteboard. He had mentioned no names, only giving initials and she thought now that he had been wise. The headmaster had said it would save him being sued for slander but Bryony understood it was darker than that. To name them would be to put a target on his own back. She looked at the inked in initials, could see her hand that day as it traced the lines.

At the top of the tree, the ringleader, mastermind OK. She had made notes and abbreviations for Transport, Logistics, Electronics, Security. A robbery encompassed quite a skills base. She looked over the initials on each branch of the tree. JL, BHH, IR, HH, JK, WW, AD, HB. She had made a particular note by the IR initials, "(*major domo*)". She smiled, it wasn't a phrase she had ever heard before DS Fox used it that day. With the last of the rubbish sorted into a bin bag she hesitated to let the Cruickshank family tree follow. She wasn't sure where it had led her. She scrumpled it up and put it into the bag with the beads and the tickets just as her mother called up the stairs.

The scent of her mother's cheese on toast made her stomach grumble. Today there was a crustily browned scorch mark on the top of the thickly sliced cheese.

"The oven melted it perfectly." Her mother took a nibble from her piece as she reached for the jar of pickled cucumbers. "It's that cheddar from the farmer's market.

Oh, did you hear about that Damien Hirst thing at the Radcliffe Collection last night?"

"Damien Hirst thing?" Bryony was rinsing out their mugs.

"Yes. Some bigwig unveiling. That awful King bloke has bought a Damien Hirst for the gallery or something. It was on Spotted In. Hang on…I'll just…" Her mother tapped at her tablet, "I was thinking about Romilly and how upset she must be after doing all that painting…" her mother swiped at the small screen. "Oh the bloody wi-fi…Ah. Here it-" her mother stopped. Bryony, reaching into the fridge for the milk turned and caught the headline.

It was only later, wrapping some crockery in old editions of the local paper that the face of Owen King kept cropping up for Bryony. Here he was planting a tree; opening the dogs home; founding an art prize; gladhanding some Twintown ambassador; winning a trophy at the golf club; financing a new restaurant at the harbour.

"I'll take these down to the car shall I?" her mum came in "Tip? Or Charity?"
Bryony nodded at the clothes bag "That's the charity one. The other's the tip." And continued reading about Owen King and a famous film star, filming nearby, arriving at his casino in the city. In the photo the film star looked awkward. Caught out. She could hear her mother opening the front door. Owen. King.

"What is it you're looking for?" they were standing by the car, one more of the bags destined for the tip was being disembowelled. Bryony had unfolded and discarded countless bits of paper and was despairing. At last, after only ten minutes, she retrieved the scrumpled up scrap she needed. Once her mother had set off for her bag drops Bryony sat in the quiet of the kitchen and flattened out the old paper.

OK. Ringleader, moneyman. This person, at the top of this tree, had the cash to fund the Cruickshank & co robbery. OK, Owen King. It seemed very obvious, Bryony thought, but equally, Owen King's most recent life exploits had been in her mind, catalogued in the local news. There was another term that DS Fox had used that day 'hide in plain sight'. It was not something she had heard before and it had struck some inner chord with her. She had parcelled it away with other phrases she liked at that time, such as 'sleight of hand'. This person. At the top of this tree. And she recalled what Romilly had said of her sitter.

37

Fox's Den

2019

The bungalow was at the very edge of Little Midham and, thanks to the high beech hedging, was in a secluded and private setting. Behind she could see the trees of Mouse Wood rising up.

The gate creaked as PC Bryony Wolfe opened it and stepped onto the path. It was a long thin tarmac strip, broken in places and sprouting plantain and dandelions. The lawn was unmowed, almost a meadow of daisies and buttercups. At a glance you might think no one lived here.

She walked up to the front door and rang the bell. She couldn't be certain that she had heard it ring out but she waited for a moment. It was rather lovely in the little porch with the architrave looping around to frame the view. No one answered and so she used the brass doorknocker. The sound rattled out into the porch itself and as she let it fall for the third time the voice behind her made her jump.

"What are you doing here?"
His face was just as serious as she recalled. He took in the uniform.

"I'm PC Bryony Wolfe sir. I've come to talk to you about the portrait unveiling at the Radcliffe."
Fox was unblinking.

"What's that got to do with me?" he was standing right behind her so that she could not move past, even though, thanks to the severity of his manner, she felt like running away.

"I wanted to talk to you about a possible

connection with the Cruickshank..." she held his gaze. He blinked at last and raised a hand to fob her off.

"Gave that game up a long time ago." He stepped back. He was carrying edging clippers. Bryony began to reach into her pocket.

"Can I just...please can I just show you this..." she unfolded her schoolgirl notes. Fox took the scrap from her, scanned it and shrugged.

"Is it a recipe or something? Some chemistry thing?" he turned it upside down and then looked up, dismissive.

"It's the Cruickshank & Co family tree. In fact it is your own tree diagram as told to me in a school assembly at the Radcliffe Academy in 2012."

"What is this?" he looked angry.

"It's my notes. From the talk you gave at the school. You handcuffed the games teacher to the piano." He stared at the paper for a long moment before folding it and handing it back.

"It was a long time ago." He stepped away as if heading back around the side of the house. Bryony followed.

"Don't you think there's a link?"
Fox said nothing.

"The twentieth anniversary. That he should be killed. At the Radcliffe on the actual anniversary?"
He did not look convinced.

"I think there might be. It's a sign. As if something is kicking off." She was feeling desperate. He was a stone wall. She reached into her other pocket for the printout she'd made this morning on the office computer. "And this. I dug around and I came up with this."

Fox was impassive as he read the headline '*Asta La Vista Barby: grisly bbq at Costa crook's home*'. She was undaunted.

"And this...this is more local. A freak accident in

the joust at Leamingworth castle. Andrew Dalton." She opened out the family tree and tapped at the initials. "Look, we have OK at the top of the tree. Owen King. Then here…" she tapped at HH "This could be this Hugh Hardacre who was barbecued in Spain and this one…" she tapped at AD "Andrew Dalton. He was skewered by this Black Knight in Leamingworth."

Fox gave her a long hard stare. Bryony was not to be stared down.

"You know who they were. You didn't name them on the day, slander and danger and all of that. But it can't be such a coincidence. They're killing each other. Turning on each other. This could be a chance, your chance, to jump on them. If they're imploding they'll slip up. This is a way to close this."

Fox was silent, still staring her down. This time Bryony did not blink. After an eyewatering minute or two Fox shrugged. He looked very tired.

"I'm retired." He looked at her. "So. There's no honour amongst thieves. What a surprise. Who put you up to this?"

Bryony felt slighted.

"No one. This is off my own bat. I'm the officer for the Midhams. This is just…" Her memory glinted with river water in spate, with a rope and a bridge and a hand reaching down to grab her. "I felt a connection. Our paths have crossed before and…"

"Yes." Fox recalled it too. "The bridge. Yes. And that day I retired. I remember."

Bryony nodded, afraid her voice would crack or that she might hug him. He looked despondent.

"You told me you were 'inspired'." It sounded miserable coming from his lips. Bryony felt it echo in her own darkness. "After all that happened to you, do you still feel inspired?" Bryony felt the knife of his words pierce her chest. She couldn't breathe for a moment, felt the colour drain from her face. There were no tears, just the searing daylight heat of panic. What was she doing here? This was a mistake. She folded the paper back into her pocket, trying not to shake.

"I'm sorry. I just…I'm sorry to have disturbed you."

He gave her a measuring look and then nodded.

"I need to crack on with this." He gestured to the lawn clippers.

He stepped behind the side gate and she heard him shoot the bolt.

38

Sat Nav

2019

PC Bryony Wolfe had opted to take the long way around the Midhams this afternoon. It was partly for fresh air, the simple pleasure of having the car window open but it was also so that the breeze could blow away the cobwebs hanging around her mind.

She had been shocked by Fox's reaction to her small, preliminary investigation. She had not meant to add to the layers of abuse and ridicule that had settled over him over the years. She had gone with the intention of doing the opposite. Standing in his front garden she had felt anticipation as if something was about to happen. She had felt their connection, that he had saved her life, that now she might be able to do something for him. There had seemed to be a reason for everything. His words had felt vicious but she understood, she had wounded him first by scratching at the old scar. If anything, they were more connected. For the first time she felt that someone, outside of her family, recognised the depth of what had happened to her.

Her mind was roiling over Fox and his talk; her own history with Crawshaw; her anxiety and guilt that she had never saved Hal and Fighty Mark from his clutches. From anyone's clutches. Her knowledge that she was hiding in Little Midham, like a mouse in a hole. She saw her mother's face, the sympathy *"Who would blame you?"* And it was the truth and nothing but the truth.

The little blue hatchback was pulled in at the layby on the far edge of Little Midham. As she drove by she saw the man sitting with the door open, his battered face drooping downwards as he perused an actual paper map. She drove on, thinking that she preferred maps, that the sat nav she had thus far used sent you on odd routes in roundabout directions. She recalled the milk lorry being snagged into the wall at Wildcote only six weeks ago, a newbie driver following his sat nav back to the dual carriageway.

    She pulled up at the crossroads at Toll Cottage. Wait. Didn't she know that car? Wasn't that Henry's car? No. Couldn't be. So many cars these days looked alike. She took the left hand arm of the crossroads and circled back around. The hatchback was still in the layby and the gentleman was still engrossed in the map. And she wasn't wrong. That was Henry's car, it wasn't just the number plate which she knew by heart, along with most of the number plates in Little Midham, it was the dinks and the prang. She rolled past once more and up to the crossroads to swing round and back again, this time via the old farm road. Yes. Still there. This time she pulled in a little way behind. The layby had room for four cars on account of it being next to Tumpey's Foot a scheduled ancient monument.

    The man who was not Henry did not look up at her approach. He was turning the map to try and orientate it.

    "Can I help at all sir?" she asked, trying not to sound like an arresting officer. He looked up. His face was bruised, the left eye almost swollen shut and it looked as if he had stuck his eyebrow back on with a bit of sticky tape. The stitches holding the skin of his cheekbone together looked as if his Nan might have done them at a crewel work evening class.

    "Is everything ok?" she had unconsciously rested her hand on the pocket for her retractable baton. The man was shaking his head.

    "Nope. I'm lost. Looking for Little Midham?" she

could understand how he might be lost. It was impossible that he could see out of that left eye. She was brusque and businesslike in giving him directions to the village. Then she drove off, taking a short cut that meant she could wait in the village to see him enter.

The little blue hatchback drove past her some fifteen minutes later. She watched as it pulled in awkwardly in a spot near Henry's house and the battered man turned in at Henry's gate. It was clear from the way he fumbled about in the pots that he had no idea that Henry kept the spare in the gnome's wheelbarrow but eventually that was the only place he hadn't looked.

He emerged from the house moments later to retrieve a box of groceries from the back of the car. She was one hundred percent sure that was Henry's car. She was also 100% certain that something bad had happened to Henry.

39

On the Third Day

2019

No one thought twice about it when Bryony took a fortnight's leave of absence. There was nothing much going on in the Midhams anyway so it was not as if anyone had to cover for her. She was moving into her cottage and that was excuse enough. Had anyone questioned her more deeply she was ready to head them off with hints about her stabbing and recovery. She could be having an 'episode about her incident' as her therapist had once put it.

She needed to find out what was happening with Henry. The way that she carried this out was to use the house opposite to Henry's as a surveillance post. Lavender Cottage which had no lavender but did have a dried up hanging basket was a holiday home and Air BnB. The owners, Marcus and Fliss texted her whenever visitors were expected so that she didn't arrest anyone for breaking and entering when they were just on their holidays. She was also an emergency keyholder.

Well. In Henry's case, this was an emergency. She took her own binoculars and settled herself in the front bedroom to observe.

It was three days before he emerged. She had, he realised, been healing, keen to be out of sight with his Frankenstein stitches no doubt. His eye was down to normal seeing size and he was quick to get into the car and drive off.

Bryony was in her car and in pursuit inside five minutes. He could not go very far or very fast due to the winding nature of the local road network. The cows would not be a hold up but if Declan was coming down in the Post van he might get delayed. It was a good three miles before there was a turn off to tell her which direction he was headed.

He took the right at the crossroads, the hatchback just disappearing from view as she rolled up. He was heading into the market town if he was going that way. Bryony took the straight ahead route, much the quickest way, but you only knew that if you lived here.

There were several blue hatchbacks in town of course, but it was not all of them that carried Henry's signature scars and the number plate. All Bryony had to do was wait.

Ivo parked in a sidestreet on the edge of the town. He had a wallet full of cash taken from Henry because he had to be off grid.

He'd gone to the outdoor shop with an idea of exit strategies. He needed stouter footwear. He needed less citified clothes. He wasn't sure there wasn't blood on his overcoat which was why he'd fed it to the woodburner in Henry's sitting room.

There was a helpful assistant in the hiking shop who Ivo could not shake. The boots on offer here were expensive. He tried on a coat and wondered why everyone who hiked or trekked chose to wear such fluorescent colours. He looked like a radioactive lollipop lady.

"It's so you can't be lost..." the helpful assistant smiled out the information "So that the rescue helicopter can spot you."
It was the opposite of what Ivo needed.

In a grubby looking market hall he found an army surplus store but at the last moment ditched the idea. The man at the counter, clad in a vibrantly beige camo bodysuit, seemed a potential danger. He would remember

Ivo. He would recall the bruised face and the cash. He was that sort because he probably took notes about all his customers ready to report to GCHQ. He would remember their interaction.

The old lady in the charity shop was having a telephone conversation about a hysterectomy and so paid no attention at all to Ivo searching the racks. The charity shop proved an excellent choice. He found two pairs of serviceable hiking trousers and a woolly jumper with a zip up collar. There was a choice of waterproof jackets. He pulled on a more subtle forest green in extra large and realised that not only was it a better, less alarming colour, it also looked worn in, less brand spanking new. This was the way to blend in without the use of camo or khaki. Only the boots seemed a problem. There was no end to the supply of ridiculous heels and vintage slingbacks in a style the Queen might wear. There was a selection of smelly trainers and some tweedy slippers, that, judging from the stained insoles, the donors had died wearing.

Further into town there was a discount shoe store. The boots were not hikers strictly speaking but they were strong and serviceable. Further along the street the very last shop was a junk shop and in the window, as if they had been put there for Ivo, was a pair of almost state of the art binoculars.

He returned to the car, watched the tubby traffic warden giving the car in front of the hatchback a ticket. He had a camera and for a moment Ivo wondered if Henry's car might be visible in the back of the picture. The car, Ivo realised, would give him away. Even now they might be looking for it. He sat for a long time pondering the problem. At home in the city the solutions were many and easy; there were always cars to steal and swap out. He knew who to go to for a paint job. Here in the sticks it was different. You couldn't steal a car, it would be too obvious and so his mind ticked along trying to find the solution. He turned back towards the market place and sat in a coffee shop so that he could see when the traffic warden had done his rounds and moved away. He needed the coffee, the blank space to think. The solution came when the girl at the counter took out a white pen and rewrote the specials menu.

He drove back, pulling in at the layby he had pulled into that first day, in order to solve his number plate problem. The permanent marker, bought from the Pound Shop, did a perfect job of making the F into an E and the 3 into an 8.

It was all very satisfying, being so hands-on and do-it-yourself. If you could stop your hand shaking while you did this, of course. This was a measure of how frayed he was by events. This was it. The whole game was played out and he must regroup. Ever since, twenty years ago, Owen King had set him the task of keeping track of everyone he had known what the endgame would be. It was as if a weight was lifted and yet somehow that weight had been grounding him. Now he felt light headed, adrift.

There was, he knew, a justice in the way the twentieth anniversary had spooled out. The backdrop of the Radcliffe Collection, the date and timing. Everything about it was a message. Now, with this last event he must take a breath. Henry's cottage was the perfect bolt hole. It was the hideaway he needed so that he might sit and breathe at last and work out what the hell he did next.

40

All of Them

2019

Mrs King had been inconsolable at the Radcliffe Collection, quite rightly of course. PC Holt had proper puked when he arrived which hadn't helped anyone but equally, couldn't be helped. Her cries had echoed around the room like some kind of sonic weapon that debilitated and disorientated. The guests stumbled and milled about under its diatonic waves as if incapable of finding the exit. He could not escort her from the building because she wouldn't be moved. She was down on her knees in front of the terrible artwork and when Holt had tried to gently nudge her to her feet and take her out she had flown at him like a cat. Like a lioness in point of fact. A predator, cornered. He wasn't sure his right ear was going to survive the ordeal.

In the end it was Havers who had come in, picked her up bodily off the floor and carried her to the back office. Which just shows that working out at the gym lifting those weights does have some purpose.

Holt had made her a cup of tea while they were waiting for victim support. He tried to take a preliminary statement. Mrs King had screamed at him, he wasn't sure what but it was like a banshee. Then she'd started sobbing which was terrifying and primal. He'd seen women cry before but not like this. It looked like her face was tearing in pieces. He would not be unhappy when Noleen turned up. She could deal with anything. The woman was a tank.

It was Noleen who calmed it all down. Noleen spoke quietly and clearly and Mrs King sat, hiccupping out her grief and giving a clear statement of the events leading up to the, well the event. Mr King had been out playing golf. Mr King had not come home. She had gone on because they were late and she assumed he had a plan. He always had a plan. Mr King was a strategist.

"We are doing everything we can to find out what happened." Noleen's voice was very soothing. Except Mrs King didn't look very soothed now. Her face flared red, little beads of sweat were bursting out of her. Even from his position by the door PC Holt could see she was shaking.

"Find him. Find him. Find him." She was spitting the words, little fizzes of spit in the corner of her mouth "He's killed them all. All of them. He's killed them." Did that make sense? Noleen cast a quick glance at Holt as if asking him the question. It was like she'd read his mind.

"Killed them all? What do you mean by that Mrs King? Who killed who? All of who?"
Mrs King turned ashen white, possibly a bit green, she looked as if she'd stopped breathing for a moment.

"Mrs King, do you know who killed your husband?" Noleen frowned. Something happened to Mrs King then, she gave a sort of spasm and she had that look the cat had when it knows you're trying to lure it into the cat basket to take it to the vet.

"FIND THEM. WHOEVER KILLED HIM. FIND THEM. FIND THEM. OH MY GOD THE SCRAMBLED EGGS. THE SCRAMBLED EGGS. AaaHHH." The banshee wail started up again and her face was almost purple with emotion.

"We will do the utmost…" Noleen's voice was like a subsonic hum beneath the keening and wailing. The utmost would be done to bring the killer in, after all Councillor King was pretty much the King of the city. I mean, look at all his charity work.

41

Quiz Night

2019

Bryony had not followed the man all day in town. She had spotted the car and then swept the main streets only to find him coming out of a charity shop. She'd had to be careful because it wasn't market day and there were not so many people that she could not be seen. After the charity shop he was in the shoe shop and then headed back to the car. The traffic warden had spooked him and as he holed up in the Coffee Pot Bryony headed back to her own car. She would get back to Little Midham and await him there.

He had bought new clothes, or new to him at least and then he stayed in the house for another afternoon. There was nothing she could see that was suspicious. It was unlikely that this man would be parading his villainy anyway. He hadn't gone into the charity shop to buy a sweeping black cape and a top hat or anything. He had bought, she could see, a disguise. He looked ordinary whereas the suit and overcoat he had arrived in had been very much city wear.

Later that afternoon she walked along Henry's street to take another look at the car. She was full of self doubt, even though his number plate was tattooed into her brain and she felt edgy about Henry. The dinks and prang in the bodywork were proof. She felt justified. But was she being overly suspicious. This man might well be a friend, she was being unjust. Henry might have let him use the house as a getaway. He might be a friend in need. As the thoughts swam she glanced once more at the number plate.

It had been altered, albeit carefully, the 3 to an 8

and the F to an E. She kept walking, her heart riffing like a snare drum.

In the kitchen at her mother's house she unpacked the box containing the crockery. It was in here somewhere. What had she been wrapping with it? That lid for the…yes. Here. She unwrapped the newspaper, looked at the photograph of Owen King in his casino with his kidnapped film star and the face of the man just slightly to the left.

Ivo had assumed that on a Tuesday the pub might be quiet. He had reckoned without Quiz Night, the notice for which he had failed to see until it was too late. There was no escape. If he turned on his heel and left that drew attention. He'd be seen as suspicious at worst and grumpy at best. They'd all talk about him probably, there was nothing else to talk about. The first question on the quiz sheet would be 'who was that bastard?' If he stayed no one would care. He ordered a pint and took up a seat in the corner by a couple of older ladies.

"You're staying at Henry's." the shorter of the two with a grey bob spoke. Ivo felt it was like a cosmic prank being played on him. He was being tested. The two women looked at him. The other woman had her hair in a sort of candy floss tempest round her head and had paint ingrained into her hands. "You old friends?"

"Or new friends. Don't be nosey Drew. I must apologise for my friend. She has an eye for a man who looks like a scuffed up pirate." The woman took a sip of her pint of porter and winked at him. The bobbed woman, evidently Drew, was outraged.

"Romilly , how can you be so…."

"Forward?"

Ivo had recovered his wits and gave a charming piratical smile. He chinked Drew's glass and the painter one with the hair laughed like a drain.

"So you're an old friend of Henry's?" the painted

one had a very direct look. Ivo regrouped once again.

"Very old. Known him man and boy." He didn't have to lie, anything he said, well, almost anything, was the truth. A younger woman approached, serious faced and almost not able to look at him.

"Bringing in a ringer then, Drew? Hey Romilly." the young woman leaned in to kiss the painter woman. She seemed to be joking but there was an edge to her. Ivo put it down to his animal magnetism. There were not many younger men in the village if this crowd was anything to go by. The collection of greybeards and wrinkles suggested a Wizard's convention rather than a quiz night.

"This is Henry's old friend…oh er I didn't ask your name, how rude of me…" Drew gestured towards Ivo.

"Ivo." He offered a hand to all. As he reached for the younger woman's hand the painter woman introduced her;

"This is our local poli…"

"I'm Bryony." She cut the older woman off. "Do you have a speciality?"

It wasn't flirting. He couldn't work out what the edge was. He shook his head and used his most charming smile.

"I'm a good all rounder."

The quiz trotted along. Some of the questions seemed worthy of University Challenge but Ivo's team, for that is how he regarded it now, had rich seams of knowledge. In between questions they chatted. It seemed the painter woman was not decorating but was in fact a local artist. His heart froze when he heard that she was Romilly Carew.

"Oh I don't deny the whole thing was shocking and terrible. I was there for heaven's sake…but that portrait. The one I painted not the whole…other…thing. That portrait was my masterwork. I painted out of my

skin and now. Well." She raised the rest of her porter in a mournful toast "It'll be consigned to the basement at the Radcliffe, never to be seen again."
Drew sighed.
"I'm not so sure. It got a write up in the paper. Didn't it go viral too on the spiderweb?"
Romilly broke into laughter.
"Oh god Drew. You and the spiderweb."
Drew grinned.
"It's very apt. We are all drawn into its strands and trapped. Anyway your portrait will have that Grand Guignol appeal you know Romilly." She said.
"It's probably worth a million already just on the shock value." Bryony suggested. Romilly looked unconvinced.
"Perhaps his wife will make you an offer for it?" Drew suggested.
"You know there's already talk of a memorial Owen King Gallery at the Radcliffe to commemorate his civic achievements?"
Romilly rolled her eyes.
"The irony." She took in a deep and weary breath. "I may never go in that building again."
Ivo's heart was a flywheel. He thought of Owen King, the very last time he had seen him. He shut his eyes.
"How is Henry by the way?" Drew asked. Ivo lurched into the present.
"He's in Wales. By the coast." Ivo blurted. It was not untrue.
"Don't suppose he recalls he owes me a tenner?" Drew was about to question him further but the quiz resumed. Ivo hardly heard the questions, his mind ticking with the bombs of Owen King and the Cruickshank & Co crew. He absented himself from the table to buy a further round of drinks and after their defeat he was quick to excuse himself.
He slept fitfully and dreamt badly. He was in the

basement of the Radcliffe on that August Bank Holiday. The dust swirled, otherworldy and the security guard loomed out of it, Ivo quick to react to jab at him and he had only meant to knock him out. The eye rolled on the floor and looked up at him so that he woke in a sweat.

42

A Knife to a Gun Fight

2019

Bryony heard the bell ring out and had no qualms about pressing her face close to the tulip glass panel and looking in for signs of movement. She rang the bell once again. There was someone in the kitchen. She had seen them move across the window. She leaned to the letterbox.

"Mr Fox. It's Bryony Wolfe. Again." She was firm and authoritative. Now she stepped back as the figure of Fox loomed along the hallway beyond. The door opened.

"What are you doing here?" He looked stern but she was determined.

"Could I step inside for a moment?" she looked at him. He was unsmiling, his hand on the door as if he might slam it shut at any moment, as he had every right to do. "Please?"

The kitchen was at the back of the bungalow and looked out over the garden. Not that Bryony took this in as she moved the remains of some bran flakes and toast and marmalade across the small table and laid out her paper evidence. Her notes and cuttings. She heard the first garbled sentence that came out of her mouth and took a deep breath before continuing. It was clear and factual.

"I don't understand. What's happened? A man stole a car?" Fox glanced at the printout she'd made at the station with Henry's vehicle details. It seemed obvious.

"Ivo Regan is staying at Forge Cottage. And Henry…Henry who usually lives there…well occasionally lives there. Henry owns the cottage. He isn't here full time. But Henry isn't actually Henry he is Byron Henry and he did mention it the other week when I was escorting him home from the pub." She took a breath.

"Are you sure you haven't been to the pub?" Fox's tone registered stern concern. Bryony nodded. She tried to focus on her breath. She felt the panic attack simmering in her chest. Turn the heat down under it, the phrase her therapist had taught her, the little coping mechanism of seeing it as a pan on a stove. She visualised turning down the heat.

"What you are saying is that this man, Henry Hallam, has loaned his car and his cottage to his probably friend, Ivor? That's what this paperwork tells us. Is it not?" he did not look convinced. Bryony gathered herself and pointed to the vehicle registration.

"No. It's Ivo, not Ivor. And yes, this is what I'm saying. You know what I'm talking about. You know who they are. You know. When I spotted him in the layby I recognised Henry's car. I know all the number plates of the locals. It had this plate." She spun the vehicle details around so that he could get a better look. "After he returned from town I noticed that the plate had been altered. The F to an E and the 3 to an 8."
Fox looked over the vehicle registration information. He looked up at Bryony.

"This Ivo man has altered the number plate?" Bryony nodded.

"So you could arrest him for same and he would be fined £1000 and the car would fail the MOT." Fox was matter of fact. "Is that what you wanted to know?" he frowned. Bryony had not envisaged this being so difficult.

"No. No." she pulled the tattered family tree from her pocket. "It's bigger than that. Look, here's the family tree again. This man is, I think, Ivo Regan. IR." She was pulling out another piece of newspaper. "Look at this photo. It's from two years ago, when they dragged this famous actor bloke into the casino, Owen King's casino and this man…This man…" she pointed at the man standing slightly to the side of Owen King "This is Ivo Regan his major domo. This man is the one staying at Henry's cottage. And Henry, who is, as you already know, Byron Henry Hallam, BHH on the tree." Bryony pointed out the relevant branches on the tree. Fox looked at them.

"Major Domo." He said, she couldn't read his expression.

"Your phrase. I wrote it down." She tapped at her family tree. "I'm right about this. You know I am. If Henry had just loaned him the car why alter the number plate? Also when he arrived at the house he had no clue about where Henry keeps the keys." Now she said it aloud to someone who was serious and, more to the point, her hero, she felt doubtful.

"Has this Henry chap reported the car stolen at all?" Fox inquired. Bryony shook her head.

"Last night at the quiz this Ivo Regan man said Henry was in Wales at the coast." The moment she said it she felt her case crumbled. It had all seemed so clear. "He's got a caravan in Pembrokeshire."

"But Henry Hallam…"

"Byron Henry Hallam." She pointed to the initials on the tree.

"He hasn't reported the car stolen?" Fox was rational. "If he hasn't reported it stolen there isn't anything you can do. No matter how many times he changes the number plate. All this shows us is that Ivo borrowed the car and has altered the plate. It's between him and this Henry chap after that. It isn't reported stolen."

Bryony felt the mental knob on the stove in her head break off.

"But this is the crew. You know it. I've worked it out. Ivo Regan is the crew. This is a chance to confront him. Arrest him."

"For what? None of this connects to the Cruickshank robbery." Fox was calm and reasoned.

"We could arrest him for stealing the car, even for just altering the number plate and then we go from there. Like Capone and the tax fraud." Bryony felt her thoughts click together and make a complete puzzle. That sounded like a plan, even out loud and in front of Fox and his steely and serious expression it sounded like a way forward. Fox gave a brief smile.

"We? I'm retired." His voice was soft and calm. Bryony looked at him.

"Do you think I'm right? Do you think there's a link?" the panic was subsiding. "I just have the initials. You know the names in full. You know all about the Cruickshank crew. Am I right on any level?"
Fox took a deep breath and was thoughtful.

"I understand your route to this. It is sound." Bryony gave a little gasp but she could see there was more to be said. Fox held up his hand before she could jump in.

"Owen King. Yes. Ivo Regan. Yes. Byron Henry Hallam. Yes. All yes. The names you brought with you the other day. Dalton. Hardacre. All yes. But." He considered his next phrasing. "I do not advise you to pursue this Bryony, not even on the most basic level. I have lived with this for twenty years. These men are ruthless. I advise you to take a step back and think. Think of the security guard, Mick Quinn." Fox's face gave a little tremor of emotion.

"He lost an eye. I understand the warning. And I understand that I was warned off once before and that ended badly." Bryony understood and she wanted to make him see her viewpoint. Fox nodded once. He put a hand on the aged bit of paper.

"What you are doing here…it is admirable…it is fine. All well and good. But…" he looked at her. "I'm sorry for the metaphor here…but what you are doing is bringing a knife to a gunfight."

43

Try Me

2019

It took Ivo one phone call to Minty in the city to discover the full history of the little policewoman.

He hadn't thought much about it at the pub quiz when she jumped in with her name but he'd realised later, in a sleepless moment in Henry's kitchen at about 3am, that the other woman, Drew or Romilly, one of them had been about to say 'policewoman' and she'd cut her short.

She had a history of shoving her nose in where it wasn't wanted. After the stabbing when she didn't die, she was shunted out of harm's way. Ivo didn't care how many times she'd been stabbed, she was clearly onto him. He laughed that the number plate was probably the lodestone that had drawn her. She knew Henry, she therefore knew his car and the number plate. His own caution and forethought had been a calamity. What a mess. What a nosey, busybody idiot of a woman. Christ. Even out here in the country you couldn't just mind your own business. He had few choices. It was eeny meeny time.

He put the key back into the gnome's wheelbarrow. He might, at some point, be able to come back here in a pinch. Certainly Henry wasn't going to be returning. It might be an idea to head back to that caravan in Wales. He was glad of his forethought of disposing of Henry's body. He had been thorough with the electric carving knife.

He thought of all of this as he set off in the little hatchback. He'd been careful this morning. Seen the little policewoman in full regalia, stab vest et al as she set off on her rounds.

Except now he kept getting glimpses of a grey hatchback following him. It was probably paranoia. On these single track, winding lanes it was impossible not to be followed by anyone else wanting to leave the village for civilisation. No. There was nothing. Nothing for a mile now. Wait. As he drove down into the dip of the road wasn't that a grey hatchback just coming over the hill behind? He couldn't see for a moment. The car scraped the hedgerow and banking making him jump. It was just thorns and branches for Christ's sake. He came upon a turn with no signage and, wary that it was very easy to get snared into the maze of lanes, he took it. He would pause and see if the grey hatchback showed up. He rumbled along the roadway. The middle of the tarmac, split open and filled with weeds and wildflowers, showed how often this route was taken. He paused under the shade of some trees and glanced back. Had the hatchback just blipped past the junction? He thought it had. Good. Either they weren't following or he had lost them.

He was lost himself now. There was no point at which he could turn and so he opted to just go with wherever the road might take him. There had to be a junction of some kind soon. Was he turning back towards the village this way?

From what he could see beyond the tunnel vision of hedge and banking, he was heading away from the village. The car bumped and ground over pot holes which had probably, looking at the state of the road, been dug out by badgers. It did not seem that you could be this remote in the twenty first century. He drove onwards, the car screaming a little in too low a gear but he didn't care. He would get back to Wales and the safety of Henry's caravan and give himself time to think out the next step.

The main road, such as it was, sliced across his view, a white van screaming by as he approached. It was going to be hard to see his way out but there was not a great deal of other traffic. He inched out right and pushed up a few gears. He was on his way. That wing mirror had taken a ding in the lanes. He opened the window and reached out to straighten it. The police car and the little policewoman were right behind him. She was flashing her lights. He sped up a little but the car's heart was not in it and besides she was pulling level with him and signalling for him to pull over into the approaching layby.

He already had the window down and she stood beside the car.

"Can I ask what speed you think you were going sir?" she said. His back was up, he knew for a fact that he had not been speeding. The two reasons were that he had just pulled out of the snaggle of lanes and secondly Henry's old hatchback wasn't up to more than forty mph.

"I was just turning out of the junction. Is there a problem, officer?" he looked at her, very direct. "The white van was speeding. If you hurry you might catch him." He remarked. He was startled by the look she returned.

"This car was reported stolen this morning." She looked him right in the eye.

"Who reported it stolen?"

"The owner. Mr Henry Hallam."

Ivo had no idea what he was dealing with now. This was the trouble with a little village he realised with hindsight, everyone knew everyone. He should have cut and run the moment he left the Quiz Night.

"Did he use a Ouija board?" he spoke carefully. She had been stabbed once, she understood the rules to the game. She did not back off.

"Can I ask what you mean by that comment sir?" there was just a little edge to her voice, a little dryness around her lips. There was something else going on.

"You do not want to try me, PC Wolfe."
And he knew it was wrong the moment he said it, he

understood in a blink that he did not have all the information.

"Thirtieth of August 1999." It was a wild card. Ivo felt his body react before he'd even thought it through, his hand releasing the door and his legs pumping him up and out and his fist clenched and airborne. Except that the punch did not land. She was like a kind of whirlwind against whom he had no purchase. She dodged and he felt the retractable baton sting his kidney as her boot rose up to catch him in his balls. He folded over but he wasn't done. From here he pivoted upwards and caught her. They slammed down hard into the road.

"Jex Lennox. 2006." She was reeling off a roll call and it was making him demented. "Ned Browne 2007. Wade Wilding 2008." He had to make her stop. It was as if they were haunting him.

"No. NO.NO." they were scuffling and scrapping and he could not get the upper hand. She was like a ferret with boxing gloves. Every blow she landed. He had to try and grab her legs. He had to pin her.

"Andrew Dalton 2009. Hugh Hardacre 2010. James Kittredge 2011. Byron Henry Hallam 2019." She had them all. He knew what was next and he had to shut her up, to quiet her before she said his own name, listed him amongst the dead. He punched her, the blow glancing across her jawbone and making her throw one of her martial arts kicks. He caught her leg and pushed her over, his hand on her throat.

"Owen. King." She croaked out the name.

"Shut up shut up shut up shut up..." she was gasping even as she was writhing. It was taking all he had to hold her despite her size. "Shut up shut up shut up." He felt her subside a little. A minute. One minute and he would be the victor. No. Kicked in the face. She was like an eel and now she was on him and calling for back up. He had no time so he must use it well. She had his arms pinned at the shoulders but his fingers could reach into his pocket for his knife.

The blood was streaming down his arm just as the little grey hatchback drew up beside. The little policewoman would not lie down, she was coming at him now with one hand filled with her guts and the other glinting with handcuffs. He was pushing her but she was trying to cuff herself to him. There would be no getting away. Distracted by his attempt to break her wrist he was unprepared for the blow from the man in the grey hatchback.

Bryony had not managed to cuff Ivo and Fox tore him from her now, lifting him off his feet. Ivo's arm sliced out, the blade of his knife snicking Fox's face. The policewoman gave a scream and her boot made contact with Ivo's leg, he felt it to the bone. There was nothing for it. Ivo struck out with the blade. Once. Twice. Three times. The old guy was sagging now and the policewoman was screaming but she was not done, the baton clipped Ivo and as he staggered back she rugby tackled him, the knife falling from his grasp, his head catching on the wing mirror so that his mind sang a high, bright note. He lashed out, his fist finding her face at last and then there was a pain in his neck. He could barely turn his head, saw the old guy in the periphery of his vision, his face splashed with Ivo's blood.

"Ivo Regan." The man spoke, blood curdled from Ivo's mouth and it was as if everything in the world switched off. Overhead, the sky wheeled, clouds scudded. The policewoman was cradling the old guy, her screams would be loud but Ivo Regan could hear nothing.

Ivo Regan was either dead or unconscious, his own knife speared into his neck. Bryony did not care. She and DS Fox were sitting in a pool of their own blood and try as she might she could not push any of it back into DS Fox. She was leaning all her bodyweight on the wound in his chest but it almost seemed that as she did that the blood gushed out through the wound in his stomach. She thought she could see his skull through the gash in his cheek. She didn't think about her own injuries, she was lightheaded, was shaking, uncontrollable and screaming into her radio now for an ambulance. Fox's hand reached for hers. He was patting her hand, giving it one lasting squeeze. He had saved her. Now it was her turn to save him.

She tried. She could hear the sirens in the distance and she tried and she tried and she tried.

44

Never Recovered the Gold
2019

Bryony gave a press conference as soon as she was stitched up enough to sit in a chair and face the cameras. It was Ivo Regan who had killed the Cruickshank & Co crew in a systematic and cold blooded coup lasting twenty years. He had been assigned this task by Owen King himself and the portrait that Romilly Carew had painted gained another notorious million in value at this pronouncement. It was rumoured that the widowed Mrs King had signed a multi million pound book deal about her experiences with the duplicitous and devious love of her life. The working title was rumoured to be '*Goldhearted*'.

Bryony was furious at the press who, after all these years, still gave Fox no credit. He had not closed the case, he had not made any arrests, the gold had not been recovered.

"No. He didn't do any of that. But he saved my life." Bryony spoke up despite a glare from the Superintendent sitting at the far end of the table. "He saved my life. Twice." She said and stood up to leave.

Bryony did not argue when she was told to take an extended period of leave. To be stabbed once in the line of duty was a tragedy;

"Getting stabbed twice, you're a liability." The superintendent had not minced words. She had been keeping up the yoga classes and her self-defence class was brimful two nights a week. Young women were coming in from the far side of the city.

"It's the publicity." Her mother said with a rueful

smile "It's an ill wind and all that."

"An ill wind?" Bryony could not stop the irritation in her voice. Her mother had been wishy washy with her of late, cossetting and coddling and it was getting at her. She felt that at any minute she might fall down into the comfort of it and never rise up. She knew that her mother was afraid of that too. She was like a human lifeboat, just bobbing alongside.

"I'm a victim." Bryony said "Are they all mad?"

"You're alive. You're here. To some people you look like a hero." Her mother's voice cracked "To some people you look like you might care, that you might have tried, that you might know what's what." It broke completely. They hugged for a long time.

Bryony was back at her cottage and just putting the cat out when the front door bell rang. She was surprised to see Jinty Matford, her landlady on the doorstep.

"Is it possible for me to come in for a minute or two. I won't keep you." And without waiting for further assent she was over the doorstep and half way into the kitchen.

Bryony moved to the kettle.

"Would you…?"

Jinty held up a hand. Bryony could see it contained an official looking letter and half guessed what was coming.

"Oh, no. Please don't bother on my account. I'm actually here on business. This is your three months' notice I'm afraid. I have to reassess my financial situation."

Bryony nodded.

"You're selling."

Jinty shook her head.

"No. I'm Air BnB'ing. It's the way it's going I'm afraid, even somewhere like Little Midham. I could have rented this cottage every week this summer if you hadn't been in it. At £500 a week minimum." She was glaring at

Bryony. "That's two grand a month if you do the maths." She looked around.

"I have no option. The last thing I need is hassle from troublemakers and…well…" She had the good grace not to look at Bryony as she spoke "Anyway, you're not going to be homeless. Didn't that policeman leave you his house?"

Bryony did not speak and after an awkward moment Jinty got the message.

Fox's bequest predated their most recent acquaintance. He had, as it turned out, made his will on retirement, about two days after their encounter at the station. Bryony was perplexed.

"I don't understand why. I didn't know him really." She was struggling with the emotion "He warned me not to pursue it. I'm basically responsible for him being killed."

"No." her mother was insistent, stern "No. That's not true. Ivo Regan was responsible for that. And if Mr Fox hadn't…if he hadn't…" Neither of them could continue for a moment. Then her mother retrenched.

"It is what it is, Bryony." Her mother tried to reason it out "If you think about it logically, he didn't have any family. It was you or the dog's home. And he did know you…he saved your life."

If it was puzzling it was also a lifesaver. The bungalow meant that she would not have to move back to live with her mum. Even Henry's old cottage, a place she would never want to set foot in again anyway, had been eaten up by the Air BnB craze. It had been bought by her landlady at a knock down price after Henry's death had been proved by the discovery of some of his teeth and an eyeball under a cupboard at his caravan in Wales.

It was fortuitous that the day she received the horrid visit from her landlady was also the day that Hayley called from the solicitors and asked if she wanted to pop round and pick up the keys to the bungalow before they closed for the day.

It was a lovely autumn evening. The golden light and the turning leaves lent a sense of tragedy and Bryony was feeling tearful and vulnerable as she made her way up to the front door of Fox's bungalow. Once again she felt the strange comfort of the little porch with its wooden architraving. She thought her heart might break as she rang the doorbell, fully aware that no one would answer.

Inside there was that faint musty scent of abandoned places and it felt empty despite the fact that all Fox's furniture and belongings were still inside. No one had come in to sort anything out, she was the sole executor and beneficiary.

She walked up the hallway to the kitchen. There was a plate and a mug upturned on the drainer from Fox's last breakfast no doubt. She tried one of the keys she'd been given in the back door. It took a few tries and when she knew which key it was she unhooked it from the fob and left it in the door.

Back in the hallway she tried to get her bearings. Stairs to the dormer. This side it was a reception room, that side a study and here another short corridor leading down to a side window and another door. She tried to orientate it. Next to the kitchen. There was a hatch in the kitchen wasn't there? So this must be the dining room. She was surprised to find the door locked. She began to work her way through the small collection of keys. Fox had certainly been security conscious.

None of the keys fitted. She looked through the keyhole at one point but the room beyond had drawn curtains. The key must be somewhere. She took a step back towards the kitchen and stumbled over something on the floor. She looked down at her throbbing toe. Beside the door jamb she was startled to see a little Chinese pottery dog. He was slightly jade green in colour, with bronze markings and made of some sort of stone earthenware. He had a rather funny, pompous look on his face. A small brass dog tag around his neck read '*Mr Chi*' in western and Chinese script. They had a name, Foo Dog guardian, she recalled.

She thought of Henry and the wheelbarrow gnome and, on a whim, lifted the dog. It was heavy. There were two keys, a larger and one smaller, on a fob sellotaped to its base.

She stepped across the room. There was a different scent in here, like a library. She drew back the curtains. It was a lovely room, looking out onto the very private garden, now a meadow of gone over daisies and valerian. Then she turned around.

This was not, after all, a dining room, despite the lovely gatefold G-Plan table with faux leather seats. It was, to all intents and purposes, an incident room. The far wall, the one opposite the hatch, carried the full and many layered Cruickshank & Co crew family tree. The Prominent Nominals here all had not just initials but full name and grained and blurry photographs, clearly taken by surveillance means. Bryony gave a little gasp. She had anticipated that tears might flood into her eyes, but instead the hairs on the back of her neck prickled. She took a step closer and began with Jex Lennox. Faded marker pen read '*identify scent*'.

Each crew member had a bio and notes and beside each, press cuttings of the murders. She looked over all of it in some detail. Fox's notes were comprehensive and included map references. The family tree was essentially the same but there was a subtle difference. She could not place it at first. Then it stood out for her; a red line, starting at Jex Lennox and winding its way chronologically around the crew as each had perished. There was a red circle around Henry Hallam and also Ivo Regan connected by a dotted red line and the phrase 'Fairview' Why did Fairview ring a bell?

When she got to Owen King there was a Post-it note over his biography. It said, in capitals, ARCHIVE BOX.

She looked at the Post-it for a long thoughtful moment then she turned into the room. The archive box that he had been carrying on the day of his retirement was sitting on the top of the sideboard.

Inside was a lever arch file filled with clear pockets. She opened it to the first page. It was a photograph, taken at the golf club, of Fox and his friend Mick Quinn. It was a sombre pose taken not very long ago by the looks of it.

The second page was a document pocket containing a white envelope. Bryony reached in. The envelope contained a plain white postcard bearing the words;

```
Happy Anniversary, defective
          Detective.
       sCrew you.
    A wellwisher.
```

There was a faint scent of patchouli about it. The next insert held mind map notes regarding women connected to Jex Lennox and three tarot shops in two nearby counties; one in Mileford, one in Wishbury and another in High Stretford. They had all been crossed out except Wishbury which was circled in red. On the following page was a heading LENNOX and a picture of three women in yoga wear outside a newly built yoga centre in Wishbury. The headline read 'Mystery donor backs Wellness Centre'.

The next pages carried notes about Wade Wilding. His face loomed out from leaflets about a security business. The location was red ringed. There was a local news story about the death of two dogs in a fancy neighbourhood and a cut out page of an A-Z with the executive housing estate marked on it. On the final

WILDING page a mystery donor had financed a Cats and Dogs Home refurbishment and extension.

KITTREDGE's last page carried a photo of the Poppy's Plot Community Farm, finance by mystery donation.

On BROWNE's final page there was an award winning wildlife photograph of the reintroduction of wolves, taken on their new Highland reserve financed by 'a mystery donor'.

DALTON's pages revealed that a 'mystery donor' had matchfunded the cost of an adventure soft play centre in Leamingworth.

Bryony's Spanish was not good but even she could work out that 'a mystery donor' had given a windfall to the Nuns of the Order of St Anthony near to where Hugh HARDACRE had been hogroasted. Bryony felt her neck prickle, felt her mind wandering down a narrow path. She could see Fox at the end of it, see his steel hard serious expression, his hand patting hers.

She turned the final page. The Post-It note said simply. LEFT HAND DRAWER. She looked at the final key on the Foo dog fob.

The sideboard, also mid-century, her gran had had one just like it, had a faint niff of sherry and cigars about it. The left hand drawer was locked and the little key opened it. Inside was a small row of gold bars. On top of them was a Post-It note saying 'Ask Mick for Instructions'.

45

Warrior One

2022

A mystery donor had funded the refurbishment and restoration of the Little Midham Village Hall. Whilst the Covid pandemic had slowed progress it hadn't halted it entirely. A dedicated group of locals, including Bryony Quinn and her husband, Mick, had soldiered on doing whatever they could themselves. Little Midham, was, after a fashion, its own isolated bubble. The contractors had been flexible and efficient.

Bryony's self-defence classes had survived lockdown along with her yoga retreats. There was no longer a police station in Little Midham. If you needed the law it had to come from the city. It did not matter much, in Little Midham everyone was community minded as well as very nosey and looked out for everyone else.

Another mystery donation had bought up the terrace of cottages at the far end of the village which were known as The Rows. These had gone up for sale early in 2020 and developers had circled. The Little Midham Home from Home project outbid everyone with the assistance of a sizeable and anonymous mystery donation. The cottages, newly refurbed, were to be rented out to local people in perpetuity and Drew, Romilly and Bryony's mum were part of the Little Midham Village Board which decided the merits or otherwise of applicants.

Bryony headed homeward. It had been a busy morning with yoga and then the Lunch club. She walked past The Rows, noticing that the gardens were all taking shape. Gnomes and fairy lights, various benches and seats had also been put out. The Rows front gardens looked out onto Mouse Wood.

She turned in at the gate of Fox's Den. The door was standing open and there was the scent of cooking from inside. Mick was in the middle of curry preparation. The aroma hit her as she stepped inside the door.

"You back?" his voice raised over the sizzle in however many pans he might have on the hob.

"And I'm hungry." She replied, as she shut the door she stooped, as she always did, to chuck Mr Chi under the chin before she headed into the kitchen and a welcome home hug.

Printed in Great Britain
by Amazon